CUTHBERT'S
Flying Circus

#5

by

Patrick Barrett

A Wild Wolf Publication

Published by Wild Wolf Publishing in 2016
Copyright © 2016 Patrick Barrett

ISBN: 978-1-907954-54-2
Also available as an e-book

www.wildwolfpublishing.com

2

Chapter 1

Cuthbert and Percy lay on their backs, hands behind their heads, staring at the clouds.

The crow flew in a holding pattern above them. *These humans are getting smart*, he thought. They had hats out of old newspapers to repel attack. Their bodies seemed to be covered in grubby material, and the little scruffy one had devices on his feet which would repel anything!

The crow circled slowly, having eaten berries all morning for this attack, but now he was getting uncomfortable. Sheering off to the side he scanned the Valley before changing direction. To his surprise he forgot to flap and dropped several hundred feet.

The apparition below him was a new one on him. *Jettison bomb load, I'm hanging around for this!*

Cuthbert decided Percy needed a hobby.

He also decided the only one which couldn't bring destruction with it was cloud-watching. The main problem was that Percy refused to see anything other than potatoes in the clouds; mashed potatoes, boiled potatoes, even sacks of potatoes.

Cuthbert banned all mention of them. It had been a quiet afternoon since. Cuthbert watched the scenes from history roll across the heavens above him. He saw the Spartans massing to defend themselves against the Persians. The rolling banks of clouds merging in combat before drifting apart, depleted. He was just watching Nelson's fleet forming a line of battle before the battle of Aboukir Bay, when Percy said, "It's an elephant!"

Cuthbert was amazed. This was the first non-organic form Percy had seen in his new hobby! Scanning the sky, Cuthbert said lazily, "No, more like a goat."

Percy was adamant and as a shadow fell across him, Cuthbert rolled onto his side.

"Aaaargh!" he yelled.

"Aaaargh" echoed Percy.

"Hroaar!" said the Elephant.

The Valley at peace was a wonderful place. Changes came over

3

people when they moved here. Henry and the Captain were seriously considering fishing at the empty reservoir where 'Whistle' sat for hours. There were no fish, but it seemed to be a really relaxing hobby.

Ronald took up flying model aeroplanes and the Valley mafia had brought in an expert on camouflage, but nobody had seen him yet!

Chapter 2

Margery, Geraldine, and Elspeth were wandering lazily into the village chatting about life, husbands, and anything else they could control, when Cuthbert and Percy burst out of the bushes and raced across the path in front of them.

The combined scream sounded something like *AaaARghhh*.

"Doppler effect," said Geraldine, "It does that."

Margery watched the duo dive into more bushes further along, and asked, "Are they wearing paper hats?"

The ground shook somewhere behind the ladies and Elspeth asked, "Anyone had a card from Arkle lately?"

Henry and the Captain reached the ridge overlooking Cuthbert's farm. Henry turned his face to the sun, closed his eyes and stretched his arms above his head. The Captain tapped him on the shoulder. Henry frowned. That could be really irritating. If the man had something to say why didn't he say it? Henry lowered his arms, opened his eyes and glared at his friend. The Captain was staring open-mouthed down at Cuthbert's jumble of buildings.

Cuthbert and Percy were neck and neck as they reached Henry and the Captain. Out of breath and tugging on separate sleeves, the two cloud-watchers tried to get some attention, but stopped to stare at the scene below.

Someone had replaced Cuthbert's farm with a huge Noah's Ark. There were animals everywhere and they were definitely not run of the mill farm animals. A giraffe was munching contentedly on Cuthbert's thatched ridge line. A flock of white doves wheeled above. The men stood silent, trying to point out the different animals to each other when they noticed the ground was shaking.

Turning as one they spied a mountain of unstoppable grey heading straight for them. The elephant, to give it its due, tried to stop. It dug both front feet into the ground and stuck out its ears. Its eyes tried to widen, but they had a real disadvantage in that department.

The men watched in horror as the soil and grass built up in front of the elephant's sliding approach. The soil wall hit them first, pushing them over the edge to send them tumbling down into the farmyard, where they landed in a tangle of limbs at the bottom of the hill. The elephant stopped at the edge and was looking for a more dignified way down.

The crow could not take his eyes off the scene. Even that irritating bee wasn't going to distract it. *Unusual that, bees don't usually come this high.*

Ronald's petrol powered model aeroplane caught the crow just as he banked for a better view. The impact knocked him sideways and he began to tumble. He assessed the damage as he fell. His slipstream made a whining noise as he picked up speed. He could understand the trail of feathers, but where was the smoke coming from? *This is it chaps, I'm about to prang.*

Looking below he used his remaining feathers to glide towards Cuthbert's thatched roof. If he couldn't make it, then it would be time for the parachute. *Uh-oh,* he spotted the design flaw! The roof came up fast, undercarriage down, air brakes faulty, not enough feathers! He hit the thatch and bounced twice before coming to rest. *Free drinks in the mess tonight chaps*, he thought groggily as he turned on his back. His beak fell open. He was surrounded by beautiful white crows. He was in heaven! Then he passed out.

Margery, Geraldine, and Elspeth rounded the hill just as the men were falling about in the mud trying to untangle themselves.

Margery tutted, "Don't they ever grow up?"

Elspeth trilled, "Ooh look! Cuthbert must have re-stocked his farm off the internet."

Geraldine took in the scene and felt a slight tremor in the ground. Sometimes she thought it was the Valley having a laugh.

Cuthbert, Percy, Henry, and the Captain were strolling from one strange sight to another. After being chased out of the mud by a hippopotamus they were hard to shock.

Percy stood before a gaudily painted trailer with iron bars. "Look at the feet on that!" The others looked over at the lion watching Percy carefully from behind its bars. "My mum served dinner on meat plates that size," said Percy.

The lion looked back at Percy, thinking, *My mum brought me meals **your** size mate.*

6

The men didn't comment. Perhaps it was the thought that Percy had a mum. A spare trailer seemed to hold the food supplies, but there was only a loaf left in it.

"Hah!" snorted the Captain. "Bread in captivity no doubt."

After a while things began to seem relatively normal. For the Valley anyway.

Percy had a little friend. The parrot lodged on his shoulder and developed the habit of nodding wisely whenever Percy said anything.

Geraldine fed the doves and now they followed her everywhere, perching on her shoulders and eating out of her hand.

Margery found a Shetland pony and groomed it to perfection.

The Captain was adopted by a marmoset monkey and they chattered away to each other.

Elspeth was trying to teach a koala bear to help with the dusting and Henry was fascinated by the chocolate brown eyes of a llama.

Cuthbert was miffed. This lot seemed to have taken over his farm and yet he didn't have a pet. Every time he approached anything it either stared blankly, or in the case of the possum, played dead.

He tapped politely on the giraffe's knees, but it didn't notice. The camel was eating a huge thistle and the lion simply licked its lips. Cuthbert stood in the middle of his farmyard. It looked exactly like a circus, except that there was no Big Top and the farmyard was square instead of round. Plus, there wouldn't normally be a house involved.

He brought his scattered thoughts under control. Why did he always distract himself and end up arguing with the other half of his brain? There! He was doing it again.

"They can't stay here," he shouted louder than intended. Everyone and everything turned its eyes in his direction.

"Why not?" questioned everyone.

"You've got barns," said Henry.

"You have fields with fences round them," said Margery.

Something squawked, "Cuthbert's jealous!"

Cuthbert swung around to face Percy. "Who taught him that?"

Percy raised his arms, the parrot raised its wings, they both shrugged.

Later in his kitchen Cuthbert apologised to the back of Percy's head, but he was ignored. Whatever his friend was eating he was making a

7

right old noise with it.

Cuthbert pressed on. He hadn't meant to shout at anyone, but all his life he had tried to have a pet. The only ones who stayed around were the dead ones. That's why he became an undertaker.

The door swung open and Percy entered with his parrot. "Calmed down yet?" he asked. Then said to the koala eating a carrot, "Move up you."

Chapter 3

The next morning Cuthbert opened his door to a surprise. Out of all the creatures which may have been waiting to be fed, he was confronted with Mrs. Biggle.

"There's an urgent telegram for you Cuthbert," she said.

"Oh, thank you," said Cuthbert, holding out his hand.

Mrs. Biggle was shocked. "It's not here silly boy, it's at the Post Office. I am not the postman, I'm the post-mistress."

Cuthbert had to ask, "What's the difference?"

Mrs. Biggle drew herself up to her professional height, saying, "Well for a start, the postman walks all the way up to your house and hands you letters. I don't, because I run the Post Office and I am on my own."

Cuthbert said, "So it's still there?"

Mrs. Biggle sighed and took out her powder compact. "I'll find out." After shouting into her compact and covering Cuthbert with white dust, she announced, "There's no-one there. I'll go and look," and off she went muttering, "If you want a job doing well, do it yourself!"

Cuthbert went back inside and Percy, noting the white powder, asked, "Was that Mrs. Biggle?"

"No, Percy," said Cuthbert wiping his face, "It was a flour grader!"

Percy and the parrot shrugged. "That's odd, she said yesterday that there was an urgent telegram for you."

Cuthbert put out his hand again, relieved. "Thanks Percy."

Percy looked at his hand, "I haven't got it, she said it was for you."

When Cuthbert left the house to fetch his telegram, his yard was full of locals feeding various animals and birds. Geraldine was surrounded by white birds, and one black one which seemed to be limping. Cuthbert eventually entered the Post Office. It was empty apart from Mrs Biggle.

Glancing up, she said, "Be with you in a minute Cuthbert; very busy this morning." Cuthbert moved forward to the counter and the post-mistress looked sharply at him. "Have you pushed to the front?"

Cuthbert stood outside with his telegram. These were a rarity in the Valley. The locals found them confusing. Instead of a full stop, they used the word *stop*. The main problem arose when someone declared

9

war on someone else and everyone in the Valley received one. It said 'Urgent-stop-form defence-stop'. After a meeting at the Mandrake Arms the majority verdict was 'If they want us to stop, we may as well stay', so nobody went.

By sheer coincidence theirs was the only village without a war memorial. Cuthbert was busy tearing open the message and he didn't notice Mrs. Biggle close behind him. He scanned the letters before him. They always reminded him of a ransom note cut out from a newspaper.

"Who on earth is Aunt Edith?" he wondered.

Mrs. Biggle went pale. Backing into The Post Office she was blowing clouds of dust everywhere as she tried to call someone urgently.

When Cuthbert's friends assembled around his table that night he read out the telegram. "Cuthbert - (stop) - your legacy - (stop) - mind lion - (stop) - stop at nothing - (stop)."

"Does the Post Office do this deliberately?" he asked. "Who is Aunt Edith?" He still hadn't fully recovered from having an 'Aunt Liza' and the adventures that entailed. "Who is Aunt Edith?" he asked again desperately. No-one at the table could answer. Percy and the parrot shrugged.

Margery coughed softly. "I brought someone with me," she said. Margery led Mrs. Biggle out from another room and found her a chair. The Koala growled at being moved again.

Mrs. Biggle wasn't used to speaking to people without a wire mesh between them. She thought of holding Cuthbert's tea-strainer up to her face, but these single men never cleaned anything!

Margery prompted her with a nod and the post-mistress began. "Aunt Edith was your mother's sister," she said, stating the blindingly obvious.

Cuthbert interrupted, "I thought that was Aunt Liza?" A shudder ran around the table.

"They both were," Mrs. Biggle frowned. "Your mother was a saint Cuthbert, a real saint." Cuthbert beamed. "But she was a terrible, terrible actress."

Cuthbert was appalled. "But she was the mainstay of the local theatre company," he protested.

The post-mistress looked him straight in the eye. "That was because we were the only one's who would put up with her. Basically,

10

we were all as bad as each other." Cuthbert's shoulders slumped. "However, Edith was brilliant. There wasn't a role she couldn't master. Talent scouts came from all over the place, but she didn't care about the craft. She saw it as 'Play-acting' and refused to believe that a grown-up could earn a living at it. In the end, she ran away and joined the circus."

Cuthbert sat up, "Which, the one out here?"

Mrs. Biggle nodded. "Probably, she had a real head for business that one. Started out selling tickets and ended up owning the lot, took the circus all over the world and made a fortune wherever she went."

Everyone reflected on this until Cuthbert asked, "Well, where is she now?"

The post-mistress shrugged, "Nobody knows. There have been strange people asking for her over the years. Even Aunt Liza couldn't find her."

The shudder ran around the table again. Mrs. Biggle became sombre, "Perhaps she has come to the end of the road less travelled, and thought she had left her circus animals in good hands."

Cuthbert swallowed hard as Mrs. Biggle stood to leave. "You mean she's dead?"

The post-mistress paused in the doorway, saying wistfully, "I doubt it. But she never could stand 'mucking cages out' and probably left."

Cuthbert hadn't considered being the owner of a circus. He only borrowed a horse when he needed one. In fact, keeping an eye on the crow was taxing enough!

Now every time he left the house dozens of gazes followed him from all heights and angles.

The whole farmyard had become territorial. The Hippo claimed the mud hole. The doves claimed the roof and the zebra stole Cuthbert's football, perhaps it was the striped jersey it was born with.

Henry and his friends were incredible. Even Cuthbert didn't know where some of the animals had been put. Food of all types was dropped off and the Valley mafia had a side-line in selling specialist manures to the cucumber farm in the next valley.

There were some very pretty ponies which Margery and the ladies groomed religiously. Percy was popular when he cured an ailment for one of the ponies. When Cuthbert asked him about it, Percy and the parrot just shrugged. "My father could always help horses in his time,"

11

was all he said.

Cuthbert was impressed, "Was he a 'Horse Whisperer?"

"Oh yes," said Percy, "He always had a bad throat. Forty cigarettes a day man he was."

The parrot nodded wisely.

Sitting upon bales of hay, the friends passed around drinks and sandwiches. Henry asked, "Was this the sort of legacy you expected, Cuthbert?"

Cuthbert thought for a minute. "I hadn't heard of Aunt Edith until this week, and I don't really see how this mangy mob can be called an inheritance."

The farmyard went silent, all eyes connected to many different types of brain focused on Cuthbert. A dove swooped across and stole his sandwich. The camel swallowed his bottle of water whole, and the goat eating the bale of hay beneath Cuthbert sped up and Cuthbert was promptly dumped onto the hard floor.

Margery tutted, "Now, now Cuthbert, animals have feelings too."

Cuthbert spotted a monkey fiddling with the latch on the lions cage and apologised to everybody of all race, breed, gender and method of perambulation. In other words, all that spits, bites or slithers! The farmyard settled down to an uneasy truce and a bruised bum.

The nights were strange. The old place had more than its fair share of creaks and groans. The owl hooted and the mice scuttled, until the snake found them anyway. Cuthbert now had to settle down to the roar of the Hippo mourning the loss of the day. The doves cooing as they mourned the loss of the light and the lion roaring as it mourned the loss of someone to eat. Cuthbert tossed around in his big four-poster bed trying to shut out all the different sounds, especially the ones coming from the room he was in.

People seemed to be missing from Cuthbert's life at the moment. Percy was wrapped up with his parrot, literally as it slept with its wings around him. Ronald was flying model aeroplanes on the other side of the hill and even though everyone spoke to him, Cuthbert knew that they weren't really visiting him. He had to admit there were benefits though. The chimney pot had been replaced, using the Giraffe as a crane, and the crow seemed to be spending his time in a deck-chair surrounded by doves.

Percy and his parrot stood behind several women in the Post

Office queue. Geraldine was thumbing through a magazine while they waited and suddenly gasped in admiration. Showing the others, they all 'Ooohed' and 'Ahhhed' at wedding photos.

"Doesn't she look lovely?" someone gushed. "I want my wedding dress to be just like that."

Percy glanced over her shoulder and without consulting the parrot, asked, "Do you know why women get married in white?"

"Yes," they chorused, ogling the photos.

Percy looked at the parrot. The parrot shrugged. He tried again, "No, really, why do women get married in white?"

Avril sighed, "All right Percy, why do women get married in white?"

Percy paused for effect, "So that the dishwasher matches the cooker and the fridge."

The parrot covered its eyes with a wing and Percy felt compelled to give up his place in the queue. They left, powered by the combined glare of every woman in the shop.

Avril turned to the others, saying, "Can some of you be at the farm tomorrow please? I have to do a piece for the paper on this circus freak."

Margery looked puzzled, "It only has animals, dear."

Avril asked, "Won't Cuthbert be there?"

*

Avril bought a special flat notebook due to Cuthbert's odd reaction to the spiral ones.

She kept a safe distance away from him as they walked around the farm. Someone was doing something with an animal everywhere she looked. *I had better be careful how I report that,* she thought. Cuthbert almost lost an arm to the lion. The snake pretended to be a hosepipe just to embarrass him. Then the camel trod on his foot and refused to move. The zebra seemed to be his only contact with the animal world and that consisted of firing a high velocity football at him every time he was framed in a doorway.

Avril mocked, "You have a real rapport with your animals, don't you?"

Percy however, seemed to be another matter. She noticed him listening closely to his parrot and then whispering things to the

13

animals. Next moment, all the ponies lined up in order of height, a monkey ran up their backs, jumped through a paper hoop held in the llama's teeth and did a forward roll as it hit the ground.

Everyone clapped and Percy and his parrot took a bow. Cuthbert ground his teeth together and stormed off. Nobody noticed.

Chapter 4

'Whistle' was in his usual place at the empty reservoir when Cuthbert thumped down beside him.

Cuthbert watched as the angler cast his hook further across the empty void. His hood was over his face as usual, and his voice was muffled, "Whistle not see the like of that circus of yours again Cuthbert."

Cuthbert just grunted. In the following silence Cuthbert calmed down. He told whistle about Henry and the Captain thinking about fishing the reservoir.

Whistle spat, "Typical townies! Think it's easy just because they see a local having some success. I can't have them coming up here Cuthbert, Whistle have to stop them. It would deplete the fish stocks."

Cuthbert had never seen a fish come out of here in his life. He hadn't seen water in it either. After a while he asked Whistle about Aunt Edith. Cuthbert watched the rod droop and the hood dip.

Whistle sighed. "Great beauty that Edith," he said, "Whistle never see her like around here again. Is that who sent the circus?"

Cuthbert nodded. Then he remembered that Whistle couldn't see around his hood, so said, "Yes."

The hood nodded gently. "There's a mystery then Cuthbert. Whistle find out soon enough. But it's best to be warned."

Cuthbert put his head in his hands. *Oh no, not another inheritance mystery.* He didn't need anything. Why did people keep leaving him stuff?

He turned to ask something else, but Whistle was gone. That was so annoying. Cuthbert sometimes wondered if it was really him who disappeared and it was Whistle left scratching his head. Then he stopped scratching his head and realised that it wasn't.

Cuthbert returned to the farm. Most of the animals were bedded down and people waved good-bye to him as they walked away home. He suspected that they were waving good-bye to the animals and he simply got in the way.

On his way through the yard he spotted the little Shetland pony shivering. It wasn't like Margery to not cover him up. Cuthbert had just the thing!

15

He went into one of the outbuildings and reached behind the door for an old fur coat. As his fingers closed around a tuft of stiff hair he tried to tug it free. Nothing, it must be stuck on the hook. He tugged harder, still nothing.

Changing his stance he reached to a different leathery spot where the fur seemed to have worn away. Stumbling against the door and reaching into the darkness, Cuthbert's hand pressed harder against the leathery surface. *There was a heartbeat!*

Cuthbert paused. It was heavy, it was slow and it was definitely a heartbeat. Moving his hand back and tugging the fur, he peered around the door. Two heavily lidded red eyes stared back at him! Cuthbert jumped back just as the gorilla punched a hole straight through the door near his head.

Marjorie was just putting a blanket around the Shetland pony when Cuthbert jabbered into view. A serious look of concern crossed her face when she saw the hairy arm reaching through the hole and clawing at the air. "Cuthbert! Don't disturb them after we've bedded them down."

Cuthbert slammed his kitchen door. Percy and the parrot looked around startled, then stared at each other and shrugged.

"Oh stop it you two," yelled Cuthbert, "I can no longer tell which one is the ventriloquist and which one's the dummy."

Percy and the parrot looked at each other again, tipped their heads to one side and scratched their heads. Cuthbert went to bed.

Chapter 5

Cuthbert's morning routine had always been quite leisurely.

He fooled himself into thinking he was busy, but very little of his day really made much difference to anything. Now however, he hesitated to open the shutters, it was traditional almost everywhere for a cockerel to greet the new day, but in the Valley the Cockerel had become sick of being ignored and handed the job over to the crow. Somehow being up from 'Crow-call to sundown' didn't have the same ring to it.

But now the job seemed to have been handed to the Elephant! When he blew his trumpet and announced a brand new day you damn well sat up and took notice, because if you didn't all the crockery in the house vibrated off the shelves.

Sneaking the shutters open slowly was like the introduction to old films where a book opens and the scene reveals itself in a cartoon. *This may as well be a cartoon*, thought Cuthbert as the farmyard was revealed.

The elephant was spraying the duck-pond up into the air, and the monkeys were sliding down the thatch. The lion stopped trying to pick the lock on his cage and was pacing up and down muttering to himself. The gorilla seemed to have lifted the out-building and moved it several feet to one side, but as Cuthbert watched the hippo nudged the fence across and altered the perspective again.

Moving around upstairs opening shutters, Cuthbert came face to face with the giraffe munching away at the thatch. *At least the house is getting its eyebrows trimmed*. Percy was already up so Cuthbert went down to find him. His friend was boiling kettles and frying breakfast. The farmhouse table was pushed up against the door to stop the smell reaching the lion.

"Where's the parrot?" asked Cuthbert.

Percy's shoulders slumped and he didn't turn around. "We had words last night. Things were said. Other things were thrown. He's gone to stay with the doves for a bit."

Cuthbert sympathised, it was awful when relationships failed. He tried to think of soft words and compassionate things to say, but all that came out was, "You had a row with a *parrot*?"

Percy banged the frying pan against the hot-plate and the cooking range rumbled ominously. "**How** do you like your bacon?"

Cuthbert patted his friend on the shoulder and sat down.

*

Henry sat in the bar with Ronald and the Captain.

The women had all set off for Cuthbert's with leftovers and scarves for the animals. When Henry had queried the scarves, Elspeth reminded him that 'Tiddles' had a runny eye. When he told the others, Henry said, "They've given them all names?"

"Let's hope Tiddles isn't the lion," Percy said.

Ronald chimed in, "Let's hope it's not Percy."

When the men were alone he broached the subject of Cuthbert's inheritance. "Why?" he asked, "In this day and age would anyone consider a circus an inheritance? Those animals could eat the annual produce of a small country in a month. And why only mention the lion?"

Ronald looked up from the small engine he was fiddling with, "'Cause she was barmy!"

Henry looked at his brother, "What makes you think she's barmy?"

Ronald glanced up again, "'Cause, she's related to Cuthbert."

Henry turned to the Captain, "But why focus attention on the lion?"

Ronald said, "'Cause if she hadn't mentioned that it was a lion, that idiot Percy would have planted it."

Henry sighed, it wasn't always easy to get a good conspiracy theory going in the Valley but his inner journalist needed something to wrestle with. "I still think it's a mystery," he muttered.

Ronald said, "No Henry, crop circles are a mystery. Why hundreds of men dragged slabs of granite all the way to Stonehenge to build a war memorial is a mystery. What happened to the three million pounds worth of diamonds I was guarding alone in the jungle is a mystery. Someone delivering a complete circus in broad daylight is simply, *The Valley*!"

Henry had to concede that his brother had a point.

The Captain stirred, cleared his throat, leaned forward and asked, "War memorial, you say?"

"Stands to reason," said Ronald. "All those uprights to carve the names on and at a certain time of year the sun shines right on the stone with the name of the head twerp who sent them all into battle and got them killed. Of course, the paint has worn off and the weather has eroded all the tool marks, but why else would anyone bother?"

Warming to his subject Ronald continued, "Of course, with the paint constantly being washed off, people would start adding the names of relatives who weren't even there, and this caused huge fights inside the circle, which is why some of the stones are knocked over."

Henry stared at his brother and wondered if they would all end up sounding like Percy if they stayed here much longer.

The crow was 'lying-in' because he had woken up during the night and watched his nemesis come to grief.

The neighbourhood fox had always been 'The King' around here. He prowled around at will and took whatever he needed, when he needed it.

The crow watched him many times, stealing an egg from the hen-house and a tomato from a greenhouse. If he took a bite from a neighbour's pig on the way home he would have a full English breakfast! But this time the fox spotted a slab of raw meat.

If he could just squeeze through these bars a bit further! The commotion was impressive. When a lion roars the savannah quakes! The fox was seen tearing around the bars at head height like a wall of death motorcyclist before powering through the food hatch minus his brush!

The farmyard gradually settled down again, three minutes before 'elephant call'.

Henry patiently waited as Ronald concluded that, "In the end, the weather in that part of the world meant that it was a constant repainting job and no-one could remember all the names anyway, so they abandoned the whole idea."

Henry tried to resurrect his own conversation, but Ronald knocked the aeroplane engine onto the floor where it sputtered into life and began mowing the carpet. By the time it ran out of fuel the carpet had a paisley pattern to match the flock wallpaper. The subject was abandoned for now.

The women had organised the animals into squads and started the feeding rituals. They seemed to automatically know how to handle every species. As Margery pointed out, "Every picture of Noah's Ark shows a woman somewhere. *She* is organising things and *he* is looking for his glasses."

Geraldine quipped, "Two by two eh! Did his monocle become spectacles?"

The women groaned good-naturedly as they worked. Arkle returned to the Valley the day before and she now joined the others. "How can I help?" she asked.

Marjorie thought for a second, "The gorilla seems to be off his food, but no-one can get near him. He's over there in Cuthbert's outbuilding."

Arkle grabbed a huge bunch of bananas and set off. Soon after, a wild roaring came from the building. The gorilla sounded puny by comparison! Arkle reappeared without the bananas and started moving the fence back. The sleeping Hippo smiled as it dreamt of being manoeuvred by a female of the species.

Cuthbert and Percy had finished breakfast. It was an unwritten rule that whomever finished first did the washing-up. That's why breakfast took so long.

Percy pushed his plate away as Cuthbert gave in and started washing-up. His mind was elsewhere as he talked, and he started scrubbing the plates with a squirrel which had wandered in out of curiosity and wandered back out much wetter than he was earlier.

"Do you see the circus as an investment, Percy?"

Percy considered this, "Some years ago, yes. But not now. That's probably why it's been dumped on you!" He put his turned down wellies up on the table. "When my family ran a circus, we…." Percy frowned as the door banged against the table. Getting up and pulling the table into the room, he admitted Henry, Ronald and the Captain.

Henry spoke first, "Morning chaps. Mind if we hide in here? The women are looking for labourers."

Cuthbert finished at the sink, "It might be harder work in here. Percy was just telling me about his family running a circus."

All eyes went to the door as the newcomers calculated the lesser of two evils. They sat down heavily and sighed as one said, "Go on then, Percy."

Percy sat down and shuffled, "Well, as I was saying. When my family ran a circus…"

The knock at the door caused everyone's eyes to widen. In the Valley horrible things could happen soon after a knock at the door.

Henry stood up, "Oh come on, it's broad daylight, what could go

20

wrong?" and opened the door.

Marvin Middlewick was a vital cog in the machinery of the Local authority. He gained fame in the hierarchy by proposing and actually producing a multi-national, multi-ethnic and incredibly tidy cemetery. Several local heroes helped of course, but after Marvin's self-indulgent font there wasn't room on the monument for everybody.

Marvin entered and took a seat, placing his briefcase on the table before him. Percy soon forgave him the interruption, and screwing his eyes shut, stretching his mouth and clenching his fists, asked, "How is Doreeen?"

Marvin looked at Percy, saying, "Are your haemorrhoids playing up again Percy?

"Doreen is fine thank you," he blushed. Obviously Doreen's transformation was permanent, and Percy deflated.

After distributing steaming mugs to everyone, Cuthbert asked, "What brings you out here, Marvin?"

Marvin opened his briefcase. "I thought I would tip you off about a new project in the village." He spread a map out on the table, saying, "It's the new traffic calming measures."

The silence was absolute, even the cooking range stopped grumbling.

"What traffic?" asked Ronald.

Marvin looked around the table and raised a finger, "Once a year some lunatic drives a bus at high speed through the village and kills some sheep. How that poor blind sheepdog isn't injured, I will never know." He raised another finger, "Just lately there have been reports of a tracked vehicle ferrying long boxes out of the Valley in the dead of night. They couldn't be coffins because we have a nice new cemetery up the hill, don't we gentlemen?" Curiously, he looked at Cuthbert and Percy when he said this.

Percy muttered something about *Not wanting to disturb the gravel*, but Cuthbert kicked him.

Another finger went up, "A speeding funeral hearse." Another finger rose, "A speeding mobile field kitchen." Another finger, "A police car on the pizza run." Another finger, "Low flying model aircraft…" He stammered to a halt as he caught everyone staring at his hand and Percy counting his own fingers. "Er, birth defect," he hissed, putting his hand in his pocket. "Anyway, gentlemen, the answer is a 'Sleeping Policeman' for the village."

21

Everyone relaxed. "That's alright then," said Ronald, "We'll just keep the one we've got."

Everyone grinned. Marvin was grim-faced. "Not Constable Beeching! I mean a concrete speed bump outside the Post Office, and large concrete flower beds to put bends in the road and slow you all down. I thought it only fair to warn you all."

Marvin stood, and leaving a copy of the map headed for the door.

When he reached outside Percy was in front of him. "Concrete flower beds, eh?" he said, "You'll be requiring a gardener then, will you?"

Marvin shook his head as he remembered something. Poking his head back into the kitchen, he announced, "I'll come back another time to check your performing circus licence Cuthbert," and he was gone.

The kitchen was silent as Percy sat back down.

Henry and Ronald were contemplating the road changes, the Captain was trying to calculate how many names would have fitted on the pillars of Stonehenge, and Cuthbert was allowing Marvin's parting shot to permeate to the parts of his brain where these things were stored behind a locked door. *License for a circus, what else do I need a licence for without knowing it?* He pressed his lips together and glanced around, just in case thinking was one of them!

Percy surveyed the table, "Ahem!" Once he had their reluctant attention, he shuffled and said, "As I was saying, when my family ran a circus...." The tapping on the door caused Percy to look around for wires attached to him. *How did everyone know when to visit?*

The door opened just a little and a face peered around. Its tongue was flicking in and out and it appeared to be green!

The door opened fully and a harassed looking woman entered. "Oh! Sorry, am I interrupting anything? I thought this was the ticket office." The young boy with her was dressed in green from head to foot, he even had a green hood pulled up over his head. His tongue continued to flick in and out.

Henry rose to his feet and offered the woman a chair. "We don't actually sell tickets, as we don't open to the public."

The green boy circled the table and settled, standing in front of Percy. The boy's tongue flicked out and Percy asked, "What's wrong with Robin Hood here?"

The woman waved a dismissive hand, "Oh, that's Jack, he thinks he's a lizard."

The boy's tongue flicked out.

Percy's tongue flicked out. Communication was established.

"My name is Mandie," said the woman in introduction. She made it sound like a feminist rallying cry, 'Man-die'. She looked puzzled, "I asked a large woman in tweeds if we could see some monkeys and she said - 'Go through that door there, it's a chimps tea-party. That's the ticket!' So I came in here."

Henry took the woman and her lizard outside to show them the animals.

Percy shuffled and tried again, "As I was saying…" He was met by a chorus of, "Surely not without Henry?" followed by, "I'll go and look for him, shall I?"

The Captain dashed for the door and when Percy looked around, Cuthbert had gone.

Percy sighed. It was no good looking for Cuthbert in this old dump. What had been your bedroom door last week could land you in Narnia this week! He was just about to stamp off in a huff when he realised that Ronald was still there. He sat back down and the two men eyed each other warily, as only two people who were convinced that they shared the room with an idiot could.

Ronald swirled the contents of his cup around and stared suspiciously before pushing it away. "I notice that you tied some of the animals to a fence out there, Percy," he said.

"And?" asked Percy slowly.

Ronald waved a hand dismissively, "Just noticed some strange knots, that's all; bit of an expert myself, you know."

Percy relaxed. He was always comfortable with his own expertise. "Got to know your knots when you're gardening," he said proudly.

Ronald nodded, "Same with hostages, can't get a decent ransom if they escape." He leaned forward, "So, what was that one you used for the elephant then? I would have used a bowline."

Percy smirked, "Ha, rookie mistake mate, that's a triple granny knot, that is."

The smirk and the tone reminded Ronald why homicidal thoughts and Percy always seemed to enter the room at the same time, but he gritted his teeth and queried, "We've all had two grannies, how in blazes can you have three?"

Percy shuffled, saying, "Well, I had one granny on the dad's side and another on my mum's side who always ate apples, and they taught me that knot."

"Apples!" spluttered Ronald. "What's that got to do with it?"

Percy beamed, "They were Granny Smiths."

Ronald's face began to resemble a colour chart for several different varieties of apples as he slid a garrotte out from his inside pocket.

Percy nipped off out of the back door muttering, "Then they wonder why I prefer parrots."

Chapter 6

Marvin stood in the middle of the high street.

It was, in fact, the only street, and there wasn't actually a sign calling it the high street. Marvin shrugged off the irritating thought. What sort of a planner would he be if he couldn't name a street? He looked at his plans. This was a good time to check out the details as everyone was up at Cuthbert's farm, playing wet-nurse to some wild something or other!

Pacing out the measurements he made several marks on his map. His anonymous instructions were precise. Certain areas had to be left clear so that bogus road-works could take place at a later date. His share of the proceeds had been hinted at and it made his pension blush!

A cloud of white dust crept out of the Post Office as Mrs. Biggle tried to make an urgent phone call.

Avril sat in her office. It took a while to realise the scenery had changed and that someone was standing in the middle of the road. Then she saw the cloud above the Post Office. Gotham City had the Bat-Phone, the Valley had Mrs. Biggle! Rushing outside Avril tried to imagine which questions would win her the 'Press Officers' Regional National award this year, to make her a 'P.O.R.N. Star.' Then she realised that it wasn't the questions which won, it was the answers! This sent her into another spin until she noticed the man was gone! Looking around wildly, she realised that she had walked right past him.

"Excuse me sir," she called. Composing herself, she repeated the acronym taught at the school of journalists. 'C.R.A.P.' **C**ompose yourself … **R**emember to lick your pencil - (Yuck, it's a pen!) … **A**lways be professional … **P**lace yourself in front, so that he cannot escape!

Marvin paused; the Press! Rapidly composing his features ready for her features, he asked, "Can I help you, my dear?"

Avril positioned herself in front of him and flipped open her notebook. "Can I quote you on that?" she excitedly asked.

Marvin frowned, "I haven't said anything yet."

"Oh!" said Avril.

Marvin decided to put her out of her misery. *While she was writing she wouldn't be thinking*, he decided. "Due to a recent spate of serious

25

road traffic incidents, and out of a strong sense of community responsibility, we are implementing road calming measures to the high street."

Avril closed her notebook. "Oh" she said, disappointed. "I thought you meant around here."

Marvin continued patiently and waved his arm. "*This* is the high street," he explained.

Avril was astonished, "It is?" she asked, adding, "We need new letterheads, already then." The note-book was open and she was scribbling furiously.

Marvin pointed out the sites of the new flower beds and the 'sleeping policeman'. Avril opened her mouth to speak but Marvin said sternly, "I've heard that one!"

Avril paused from her writing to ask, "Will there be a public debate?"

Marvin was taken aback, "About what?"

Avril pressed, "About all these alterations and the way they will impact upon the lives of the villagers?"

Marvin smiled thinly, "How will they affect you?"

Avril thought, saying, "Not at all, really."

Marvin was delighted. "There we are then. We have had a debate in public and it has caused no ill-will at all." He poked her notebook, adding, "Put that down dear, after due consultation with the public the plans were approved."

Marvin walked away whistling while Avril scribbled furiously.

Chapter 7

Cuthbert poked his head round the corner and found that he was alone. Retrieving his cup of tea, he went upstairs slowly. At the top of the stairs he turned towards a blank wood-panelled wall.

With a sigh he slid the panel sideways, stepped onto another set of stairs, and slid the panel shut behind him. At the top of these stairs he entered a room with a sloping ceiling.

He was right under the thatch now, and this was where all the Valley secrets could be found. Old leather-bound trunks were ranged along the floor. They contained maps, drawings, inventories, and long lost works by many of Cuthbert's ancestors. The journals were an eye-opener in themselves. From leather bound cover to leather bound end board they detailed years and years of unremitting boredom!

His ancestors may have been great journal keepers but they certainly weren't adventurers! Aunt Edith was a puzzle.

Cuthbert had sat up here for hours reading through the books, hoping for pirate ancestors or highwaymen. Sure, the Shakespeare connection was fascinating, but it wasn't family! Cuthbert knew that he had an uphill task ahead of him.

Once in every generation, someone was detailed to organise the journals into some sort of order, and of course everyone used a different filing system. Edith may be filed under 'E' for Edith or 'A' for Aunt Edith. Equally, she may be under 'C' for circus owner or 'S' for Cuthbert's mother's Sister!

Cuthbert felt the responsibility of all this weigh heavily upon his shoulders. He was now the sole custodian of all this history, and only he knew about it.

He sighed again as he moved Percy's hat and sat down.

Percy's hat!

Cuthbert stood up sharply, banging his head against the roof. "Percy!" he yelled.

Percy woke with a start and banged his head on a lower part of the roof. They stared at each other as they rubbed their heads in mirror image of each other.

"This is a secret," spluttered Cuthbert indignantly.

"No, it's not," said Percy.

Cuthbert sat again. "How did you know?" he asked.

Percy finished rubbing his head, saying, "Well, I noticed that when you were gone for any length of time it always took the same amount of time for you to disappear. I timed you one day and then tried different directions taking the same amount of time each try, all starting from where you did. Also, the candle you took with you had always burned down by the same amount, and only one route resulted in a squeaky floorboard at precisely the right time."

Cuthbert was impressed. "So you equated all those factors and using empirical methodology, found this room?"

Percy nodded, "The footprints in the dust helped too."

*

Henry slipped his arm around Margery's waist and squeezed. "The little fellow's enjoying this. Do you think we should open it to the public?"

Margery smiled. After the other animals got used to seeing a boy-shaped lizard on an elephant's back, the whole afternoon had been fun.

"It's not up to us darling," she said. "Cuthbert might not want to run a circus."

Henry noted, "He doesn't actually run anything. It seems to all run smoothly in spite of him, and besides, when you think about it, most of Cuthbert's life has been a circus."

*

Marvin pored over the maps.

As high up as he was in the Local authority he could initiate a new survey or policy at any time, and he could work unsupervised. There wasn't a single tunnel shown on these maps! He knew they were there, he had been in them. He had seen people disappear in one direction and pop up somewhere else entirely!

He studied the maps closely. There were drains, of course there were, but not many as there was only one street. Marvin scratched his head. The street didn't seem to be in a sensible place! Normally a village formed at a crossroads on the way to somewhere. It was where travellers rested on long journeys, or stopped for water at a nearby river. By the same laws of non-planning, the village would be at the

28

bottom of the fold in the Valley, so the street would be the lowest part. This one wasn't! He peered closely. Why was there a bend in the drains? They seemed to be avoiding something.

Marvin jumped as a box on his desk crackled, "Squelch! Here - 2-C- U – SQUELCH," was about as close as Marvin could get.

Pressing a button, he snapped, "Are you eating crisps again?"

The newly installed intercom was a real nuisance. A white plastic monstrosity, it looked like the box for a surgical appliance. The cable wasn't long enough for it to sit square, so his blotter looked crooked and that made his pencil lean! Why did 'improvements' never live up to their promise?

A tapping at his door put Marvin firmly back in control. "Enter," he barked.

The man who entered sideways resembled a cartoon ferret. He held a cap in his hands and was twisting it nervously. As Inspector of drains, he had been in some really awful places in his time, but nothing as bad as the office of a boss.

Marvin tapped the map imperiously, demanding, "Is this your signature?"

The man paled. Even upside-down, he recognised the Valley! "Er, yes sir," he mumbled hesitantly. "I countersign all the surveys, sir."

Marvin fixed him with a steely gaze, asking, "When were the drains first laid?"

The man laughed, "Oh goodness me, sir. The first plans were drawn with a quill. You can't blame me for that set." The laughter stuck in his throat and decided not to come out as Marvin stared.

"When was the last time they were dug up then?"

The man was taken aback, "Well, never sir. We don't just dig things up to see if they are still there you know."

Marvin tapped the map again, "Why is there a detour around something under the street?"

The cap-twisting became serious now, "Er, your predecessor asked that once sir and we went to have a look."

"And?" prompted Marvin.

"Well er, have you ever been to the Valley sir?"

Marvin nodded slowly, but remained quiet.

The man was suddenly full of information, "Well sir, me and Arthur were sent over there to dig things up and move them around a bit. The last boss only liked straight lines on his maps. We met some very strange people, sir. We ended up calling it the Valley of the zombies, sir." His voice trailed off as hidden memories resurfaced. "I never saw Arthur again, sir," he mentioned wistfully.

Marvin sat back. "What sort of people?"

The drains Inspector trembled, "Well there was this one chap who seemed friendly enough, but some days he couldn't talk and other days he would drag one leg behind him. Some days it was a different leg or he would have his sleeve sewn to his jacket."

Marvin waved impatiently, "That's just Cuthbert. He's always embalming himself."

The man began again, "There was a little chap in wellies who insisted that we weren't digging deep enough for carrots. We told him to clear off, and next day he had filled the trench in and sat and watched to see if we did it right next time. Then this scatty, young woman came over with a note-book, took a photograph of her foot and said, 'I'll see you in the next edition'. It sounded like a threat." The Inspector wiped his brow and continued, "We were getting nervous by then and when Arthur tried to make friends with a sheep dog, it completely ignored him. Then the next day, we found the trench filled in and planted with bulbs. We started digging it out when this huge woman appeared and threw the compressor out of the way. It took a tractor to get it there! Then we heard an old fashioned horn and a bus came charging down the road, the dog came to life, a flock of sheep disintegrated before our very eyes and an old woman blew a white powder all over Arthur. I never saw him again; it must have been pixie dust! I wasn't having any of that sir, I legged it."

Marvin considered. Once you had visited the Valley all the pieces managed to fit, but the end puzzle somehow never made any sense!

"Can I go now, sir? I think I would like to attend counselling again."

Marvin waved him away.

Once he had passed 'cubicle city' the drains Inspector saw a woman sitting before a white plastic box eating crisps.

"What did you think of Mr Middlewick?" she asked between mouthfuls.

The man didn't hesitate, saying, "After all my years in drains and sewers my dear, there is only one certainty in life; all the big lumps float to the top!" He left to the sound of choking.

Chapter 8

Percy's head popped up from behind another trunk. "Where's the crypt?"

Cuthbert reminded him, "Under the cinema where Mandrake Hall once stood. That's where we were trapped and you found the ring."

"Ohh, I remember," said Percy, disappearing again. He had also got his thumb stuck in the eye socket of someone's remains, but some stories don't travel well.

The two friends had been rummaging in the trunks for hours, but there was no reference to Aunt Edith so far. Of course, a methodical search may have paid dividends, but with Percy constantly side-tracking things, chaos reigned.

"Who was Captain Cuthbert-Cuthbert?" asked Percy this time.

Cuthbert sighed and explained. He was one of the few sea Captains who could write his name and he was really proud of it. Every time anyone said 'sign here', he did. Unfortunately, for his Captain's papers, they meant either, 'put your mark' or sign both Christian and surnames. He automatically signed where they said 'sign here'...'and here', and he was Captain Cuthbert-Cuthbert ever after.

Percy thought, *sounds about right*, but said, "Was he a distinguished sea Captain?"

Cuthbert said, "He should have been. He discovered America one foggy day when the voyage took longer than it should, but nobody believed him because he was only supposed to be collecting whelks from Grimsby."

Percy stared at his friend trying to work out whether this was some 'reverse-Percy-ism' but Cuthbert seemed to believe it all, so he went back to rummaging.

"Found anything interesting?" asked Henry.

Cuthbert jumped! "This place has been a secret for over a hundred years," he shrieked. "How come everyone can find it now?"

Henry looked quite affronted, "You left the panel open."

"Oh!" said Cuthbert.

Outside, listening to the men through an old pipe, Margery said, "These men really love their secrets, don't they?"

Mrs. Biggle nodded as she handed out the sandwiches. "That top

31

room of Cuthbert's came in very handy when we were children. He never could find us during 'hide and seek.' We knew about it before he did. His parent's swore him to secrecy and he thinks he's the only one who knows."

"Does he know that we can hear him through this pipe?" asked Geraldine with a gleam in her eye.

Chapter 9

Marvin sat at his desk trying to sketch out anything he could remember about the tunnels.

He drew in the places he had seen, but nothing linked up or made any sense. *Perhaps, I should commission a full survey of the tunnel system?* That would be the perfect way to disguise the planned excavation! Marvin set to work, memos to be written, plans to be drawn-up, troops to be assembled. This was the adrenaline kick he had joined the Local authority for!

*

Henry came back outside to find the women and several animals clustered around an old pipe.

Geraldine seemed to be talking to it! As he came closer, Margery signalled him to be quiet.

Geraldine was saying, "Whoever finds the secret in the forbidden papers will be rich beyond their wildest dreams." Stifling a giggle, she put her ear to the pipe.

A muffled voice came back, "Are you sure? I have some pretty wild dreams you know."

Geraldine composed herself before replying, "You could have anything you wish. Is there anything that you desperately need?" The women were falling about, but Geraldine was suddenly stricken by horror at the reply. She couldn't move because everyone was pressed up behind her trying to listen.

Percy said, "Toilet facilities up here would be nice," as he emptied his cold tea down the pipe!

Geraldine burst out from the crowd flapping her hands and spitting wildly.

The animals watched in fascination as she cleared the fence and headed for the village.

Percy clonked his cup against the pipe to knock the tea leaves out and said smugly, "They might go to expensive schools, but the old tricks are always the best."

Cuthbert was in shock. It had been up here where he met his

imaginary friend, Chester. They had only talked in this room and then he had suddenly disappeared forever. Had Percy just ruined a visit from Chester?

*

The atmosphere around the table was tense.

This was a crisis. A workman's hut should be a place to relax and be drugged by the heady aromas of stale tea, burnt toast and that pungent ointment Simon used on his rash. The air should not be tense; it should be thick like a blanket. It made the afternoon nap much easier. The drains Inspector watched the men who made up his team. Buster hadn't reacted yet - he was waiting to see what the others did. If they thumped the table, get ready to order a new one, he was a big lad was Buster.

Swivelling Simon got his name from his glass-eye. It normally stayed in its place, but whenever he panicked both eyes went in opposite directions. This panicked everyone else and the day was lost. The other member of the road gang was 'One-lung Louie'. The amount of cigarettes he had sucked to death seemed to have literally taken his breath away! He could spot an emergency with the best of them, but by the time he shouted a warning he was the only survivor!

The men were not pleased. Not only had the drains Inspector found them a job. He'd forgotten the milk!

*

Percy noticed Cuthbert sneaking back to the pipe and listening carefully.

His senses were torn between tormenting his friend and the book he was reading. The page was headed, 'Secrets of the Valley' and was blank. Now, Percy reasoned, either it was blank because everything was secret, or there were no secrets to write down, or the person who wrote the heading knew that there were secrets but didn't know what they were. Percy was thrilled. He thrived on secrets, especially someone else's!

*

34

The road gang made a fresh brew and stared suspiciously at the worksheet on the table between them.

There was no rush; no-one ever bothered them in here, mostly because they stank of whatever the last job had been, even it was finished months ago.

Simon picked up the paper and read the instructions. The others watched his lips move. Flinging the paper back onto the table he snorted, "No big deal, they want us to dig up some chap's alley."

Everyone relaxed and mugs were raised.

The door swung inwards and the drains Inspector announced, "Sorry lads, daft girl made a typo, it should read *Valley*."

Mugs never made it to mouths, faces paled, one eye swivelled wildly. Even Buster was on the front row with this one!

*

Marvin was screaming into his intercom trying to decipher the garbled crackling, when a smell oozed under his door. His breath caught in his throat and he rolled his chair to the window, flinging it open.

The door crashed back against the wall and the smell personified entered his office.

Marvin tried to focus through streaming eyes as one of the men announced, "We are the road gang. We work for the drains Inspector."

Well, thought Marvin, *That explains that then*. Turning to the window he gulped in fresh air as fast as he could, so that he could politely face them without opening his mouth.

They demanded extra men, extra pay, a completion bonus and 'those cool green vests that light up when someone shines a torch at you'.

Marvin refused to do anything which involved an intake of breath, so his frantic nodding was taken as acceptance of all their terms.

The road gang strode back through a terribly disturbed 'cubicle city' with huge grins on their faces. They considered themselves to be 'ace' at negotiating. They always got what they wanted!

*

Percy turned the book through three hundred and sixty degrees.

He held the page up to the candle for invisible writing. He

35

breathed on the page and after rummaging in his welly rubbed a slice of lemon over the paper. He even shook the book in case the secrets might fall out.

In the end he gave up in disgust. "What do you make of this, Cuthbert?" he asked, tossing the book towards him.

Cuthbert caught the book and flipped it open. "I remember this," he said. "It was my homework, I never did finish it."

Percy slumped; results were always inversely proportional to effort in this place.

*

At the sight of an attractive woman the road gang stood to attention and adjusted their brand new high visibility jackets.

Margery introduced herself as the landlady of the Mandrake Arms, and after wrinkling her nose suggested that she reserve an outside table 'just for them'. The men were charmed.

Buster was trusted to set up the striped tent while the rest of them fetched the truck with all the gear. Having set up the tent over the potential hole in the road Buster could only watch as an elephant stormed down the street, ran into the tent and ran off wearing a striped football jersey!

Marjorie came out at that precise moment to hand him a drink, not batting an eyelid.

That decided it! If she hadn't seen it, then neither had he! Putting the kettle on over a little gas stove he prepared to wait for the rest of the crew. The drains Inspector always travelled separately, he was management after all.

After spraying coded lines and symbols all over the road to mark out the site, he returned to his van to find a hippo sitting on the bonnet. Wandering over to sit in safety with Buster his overriding thought was, *Mustn't spook the crew, mustn't spook the crew.*

Further down the road Simon was driving the road roller up to the site. It needed great concentration to drive one of these, especially with one eye. Simon watched the road ahead. The road watched him right back!

The black tarmac seemed to have a bump in it, and the bump seemed to have eyes, then teeth. The gorilla began beating its chest before leaping onto the roller and pressing its face up against the glass windscreen.

Both Swivelling-Simon's eyes rolled backwards to look inside his head where it was safe.

One-lung Louie had been sent to walk over the fields laying tape where the pipes were thought to run. He was on his way back when he spotted an incredibly beautiful flower. He stooped and looked at it from all angles; then he raced over to tell his mates. Of course when he got there he was out of breath, but he had to try and tell them. All that came out was, "Hurr, hurr, hurr."

The drains Inspector patted his hand and said dreamily, "We know Louie, we know," and they all sat there in shock pretending that they were in a tent.

Chapter 10

Cuthbert's kitchen was unusually full.

This time, the women and the monkeys had decided to attend. There was a suspicion that the snake was eavesdropping, but he hid it well. "Will they find anything?" asked Henry."

Everyone shrugged, but of course the snake may have been swallowing!

Cuthbert said, "We haven't found anything to worry about."

Percy quipped, "That's never stopped us before."

The cooking range made a sniggering sound as Elspeth tried to dust it. It began to look as if it was ticklish!

The Captain spoke, "Went to the council today, pulled the old boy act and got a look at the plans. The pipes definitely divert around something, just where they're going to dig." The assembly went quiet as they all explored totally useless and diverting options.

Ronald suddenly asked loudly, "Who's the oldest person in the Valley?"

"Me!" croaked someone.

Glances were exchanged and ears tuned for a repeat croak.

"Over here," came the next croak. Squashed amongst the visitors was a shrivelled version of Cuthbert. He was no relation; it must be the Valley air. "No need to panic everyone," croaked the man. "The only reason for the diversion was because they ran out of pipes. It was many years ago and it would have meant fetching them by horseback from miles away. They had to buy some from Old Cyril and he only had bends in stock, so they fitted bends one way, then a straight and then bends back the other way." The old man crackled, "Made a fortune off them, did old Cyril." He crackled some more.

Ronald asked, "Is Old Cyril dead?"

The old man snorted, "I wouldn't be telling you this if I was, would I?"

Everyone relaxed.

Henry breathed out and said, "Phew, we can just let them get on with it then?"

Old Cyril croaked, "Yes, there's nothing at all where the diversion is, but if they dig a bit deeper, *Oh dear!*"

38

Everyone froze. "So there is something there then?" asked Ronald.

Cyril said, "Why do you think they call it *The Golden Valley*?" It was soon established that absolutely no-one had ever heard it being called anything like that.

Everyone clamoured for information until Cyril held up a weary hand. "Look," he began, "Have you heard of Eldorado?"

Henry replied, "Yes, the man of gold. Was he here?"

"No, you fool. He was in South America. Have you heard of the Golden Hind?"

Percy said, "Yes, Sir Francis Drake's ship, was that here?"

"No you fool, can you see a harbour?" Cyril was getting quite irate now. "Have you heard of some rocks deep underground which when crushed reveal nuggets of shiny metal?"

The Captain asked, "What are you blathering on about?"

Cyril snapped, "I'm trying to tell you dummies what gold is!"

Ronald banged the table, shouting, "We know *what* gold is, you silly old fool. *Where* is it?"

Cyril glared at Ronald, "Watch it you young whippersnapper. I was twice the man you were at your age, and three times the man you were before you were born."

That kept Ronald busy counting on his fingers and allowed Margery to lean over to ask quietly, "Cyril dear, where is the gold?"

Cyril smiled the winning smile he had used many decades ago to win the heart of 'whatever her name was', saying, "Why, it's just outside your pub, under the road my dear."

Henry whispered to his neighbour, "Jasper, activate the Valley Mafia."

*

The road gang were becoming increasingly paranoid. Even the bushes seemed to be watching them.

The people at the Mandrake Arms seemed to be okay, but the chap who walked like a penguin could be quite worrying.

Speaking of worrying, Louie was trying to get them all to discuss the 'wonderful things they had seen' when the rest of the gang didn't want to mention any of it at all.

In the afternoon a scruffy little chap in wellies appeared. The Inspector of drains had recognised him, but kept quiet.

39

Percy sat on the edge of the hole swinging his legs. The fumes from his wellies wafted around like some diabolical censer, and even these hardened workmen felt their eyes water. "Watcha doing?" asked Percy.

The team eyed him suspiciously.

Percy shuffled and said, "All my family have been involved in digging and tunnelling you know, right back to the first channel tunnel."

Buster took the bait, "What first channel tunnel? My dad has only just finished this one."

Percy shuffled in earnest now as tools were laid to one side and he had their attention. "The first channel tunnel was supposed to be finished before the Spanish armada sailed," he began.

"That long ago?" asked Simon, fighting a swivel which came naturally when faced with Percy.

"Oh, yes," said Percy. "The original one was going to run from England to France and be flooded so that our fleet could sail through and come up behind them. The theory was that when the French and Spanish fleets joined together in the channel and reached Dover, there would be nobody there. Everyone on foot would have gone inland and our fleet would have sailed underneath them and parked their ships in Calais, waiting for them to come back. When the foreigners found the ports empty they would have nipped back for their wives, and supplies ready for a proper invasion. But when they got back the British ships would be at anchor in place of them and all the beer would be gone!"

The road gang gaped. "What happened?" they asked, as the monkeys carefully stole the tools from around the hole and the elephant towed the road roller away.

"Well," said Percy shuffling again. "The ships were all loaded and ready, and the admiral gave the order to unplug the tunnel. The water rushed into the tunnel taking the British ships with it. They hurtled through and came out right in Calais harbour. The Admiral just had enough time to shout, *I claim this harbour for…,* when the water all rushed back the other way and took his fleet with it. This happened two or three times until the fleet was stuck in the tunnel somewhere in the middle. The Admiral needed a quick solution so he ordered all the ships to fire at the tunnel walls. Every ship fired broadside and smashed the walls. The British ships popped up like rubber ducks in a bath, right in the middle of the Armada, and scared the bejesus out of them. The Armada panicked and went the wrong way around Ireland. The rest is history!" Percy said, getting up and going for a pint.

The road gang were speechless. "What a fascinating chap, where's my shovel?" asked one.

"Never heard that story before, bet the Government hushed it up."

"Where's my pick?" said another.

The drains Inspector said, "I've seen him somewhere before!"

Louie asked, "Was I the only one to see monkeys in reflective jackets?"

*

Marvin was trying to rant and hold his nose at the same time, "How the blazes can you lose a road roller?"

The men stood shame-faced.

"Where were the tools?" he asked.

"In the hole, under the new tent," said Buster.

"Where's the tent?" asked Marvin out the side of his mouth.

Buster slumped, "The elephant took it again."

Marvin took a deep breath from outside the window and roared, "Is the hole still there?"

Buster looked at his mates for inspiration but there was none. "Do you want us to go and check?" he asked.

41

Chapter 11

Henry wasn't convinced. Cuthbert checked his records, after a fashion anyway.

Geraldine researched the museum archives and Old Cyril had fallen asleep. Henry had tried his old journalist contacts but it was very unwise to mention 'gold' to the feral packs hunting for news. He had resorted to, 'heard anything odd about the Valley' and was greeted by gales of laughter every time he tried it.

One contact had gone as far as to say, "Ring me if anything normal happens and I'll hold the front page."

The Triple Echo local newspaper's archives didn't go back very far and Avril was a 'loose cannon'. She wouldn't recognise a story until she'd let it slip and read it in someone else's paper!

Henry couldn't understand why there would be gold in the Valley. He had heard the tales about the Roman pack mules buried under an avalanche, but not even the museum had bothered to look into that one. Was it the proceeds of a crime? Again, no record of one, this was going to keep the Valley awake. Not that the circus animals were doing a bad job of that already.

*

The foggy atmosphere inside the works hut wrapped itself around the road gang. Mugs were clenched and so were lips.

New equipment was issued, but they had been sniggered at by 'office-wallahs'. They were used to being the 'hard-men' of the Local authority. The hit-men called in when only a shovel would do! Reputations were at stake.

Ordinary workers turned away when they passed by. It had always been that way. The team began to discuss tactics.

Simon closed the window, saying, "Walls have ears."

Outside a bush whispered, "Damn!"

*

Marvin dialled the special number.

The person on the other end listened, choked slightly and demanded a better result next time he phoned. Marvin sensed the weight pressing down on his shoulders.

*

Geraldine had joined Cuthbert, Percy, Henry, and the Captain in sorting out the journals.

"Could this be another Shakespeare connection?" she wondered aloud. "Maybe the Bard stored his wealth here?"

Henry replied, "Wasn't wealth kept close in those days? I would have thought it was tied up in his houses in Stratford."

Geraldine shrugged her agreement and they all resumed their page-flicking.

"At last!" shouted Percy.

Everyone looked up. He was removing a piece of bacon from inside his welly and dropping it inside a book. "Seeing everyone watching him, he said, "What? I don't want to read the same one twice."

*

Margery sat at the table in the old mill as Elspeth dusted around her. Chattering as she worked, Elspeth revealed that she had always wanted to be a career woman.

"Like that Aunt Edith," she said wistfully. "It seems that she was good at everything; she must have made a fortune!" The scrape of Margery's chair announced that she was leaving, and in a hurry too! "What is it dear? Have I missed a bit?" she asked the empty room.

The men were stretching and rubbing their eyes when Margery slid a panel sideways and entered the 'secret' room from *the other end*!

The men gaped, looked at each other, then at Cuthbert's door and then at Margery's door.

Margery sighed, saying, "The woman who cleans the pub told me about it. Get over it!" Then she sat down and put forward her theory. "The gold or money, whatever it is, must be Cuthbert's inheritance. It was built up by Aunt Edith and stashed in the Valley. Somehow the lion holds a clue, that's why she wants Cuthbert to mind the lion!"

Cuthbert said, "Maybe she meant *mind the lion* because it's a nasty

43

vicious beast with huge claws."

Chapter 12

The next morning everyone gathered around the lion's cage.

The lion, sensing a captive audience, played the 'King of the jungle' to the full. It paced up and down, emitted a low guttural growl, and its amber eyes dared anyone to come closer.

Arkle was passing by carrying a mound of hay-bales when Margery called to her, "Could you spare a moment please, dear?"

The lion had completed another leg of pacing and turned, flicking his mane dramatically, only to find Arkle pressing her face against the bars. Padding over menacingly the lion prepared the roar of a lifetime.

Arkle's hand shot out, and grabbing the lion's mane slammed its head against the bars. The cross-eyed lion slumped to the floor.

Percy ran up the short wooden steps and flung open the cage door, "Come on Cuthbert," he shouted, "Now's our chance."

Forced on by the stares of everyone behind him Cuthbert ran up the steps to where Percy was holding the door open. Percy counted, "One, Two, Three," and lurched forward.

Cuthbert moved forward too and Percy shut the door behind him! Cuthbert froze.

The lion lay on its side like an advert for syrup.

Suddenly Cuthbert was in the cage and the world was looking at **him**. *"What do I do now?"* he hissed.

Percy shrugged, "Go through his pockets, I suppose."

Moving forward Cuthbert paused for a reality check, glaring at Percy. No-one observing could offer any advice either; they were watching the lion lifting its head!

Cuthbert kicked at the straw in frustration. "Oooh! Look," he said, "Someone has scratched a huge cross on the floor."

Percy jumped up and down. "That's it Cuthbert, start digging."

Cuthbert slyly looked at him, "Hand me the spade then."

Percy snatched a trowel from inside his welly and opened the door. Cuthbert dashed past him just as a huge claw whistled past behind him. The two tumbled down the steps as Ronald slammed the door, knocking the lion out again.

"Why didn't you start digging?" asked Percy.

"Why did you shut me in?" countered Cuthbert.

45

"Because that's where the treasure is," shouted Percy.

"No it's not, that's where the lion is," yelled Cuthbert.

"You were scared to dig," accused Percy.

"Look under the wagon," shouted Cuthbert. "It's the farmyard, there's nothing there you dolt!"

Percy stood and brushed himself down. "Huh, you know nothing," he huffed. "We always marked the bottom of the boat so that we would find the biggest fish again."

Off they squabbled into the distance as the audience broke up and began the feeding routine.

Chapter 13

The road gang were almost set up. The stove hissed, the kettle bubbled, and the new striped tent flapped above them.

The bushes moved closer.

The drains Inspector paused to take in the scene. Like a Commander of old preparing for combat he registered the scrape of iron on rock as spades were readied. Pulses quickened as his men psyched themselves up to do battle with the earth itself. All of history lay below them like some historical layer cake. He prepared to give the command.

Buster was distracted, never one to be the first with a comment. He nevertheless risked his reputation as he asked, "Who moved the road roller?"

Everyone looked up. Battle-ready muscles relaxed slightly. "No-one," snorted Louie. "It's over there."

Muscles tensed and Buster tried again, "But wasn't it closer?"

The drains Inspector was becoming annoyed; Buster was ruining his moment. He would be willing to bet that Montgomery never had his 'eve of battle speech' ruined by someone suggesting that Tobruk had moved! "Buster," he said, "We took the key with us and dismantled half the engine. It cannot have moved."

Simon's eye swivelled as he said, "No, but *we* might have. Isn't the lady from the pub walking further to bring us our drinks?" They watched as Belinda rested the tray on top of a gate-post for a moment and then continued towards them.

The drains Inspector looked around in panic. They were around the stove. The stove was in the tent and the tent was on the markings. What could possibly be wrong? Crouching over the road, he squinted like a white hunter checking spoor. Scuttling along to keep the same perspective, he spotted it. "Damn!"

The bushes moved away.

Marching back to his troops the drains Inspector declared, "Someone has copied the road markings over here and parked the road roller on top of the old ones."

Everyone gaped.

Taking command the drains Inspector barked, "Right, first we reassemble the road roller, then we dig the hole, then we brew some tea!"

His men snapped to attention and moved quickly.

The drains Inspector cringed as each situation report came in.

"The engine parts aren't here," followed by, "The tools have gone," then, worst of all, "The kettle's gone," all followed by the most puzzling one of all, "Where's Simon?"

The bushes had disappeared!

*

The Valley Mafia found this one fascinating.

He was sitting on a rock and if you poked him one side his eye swivelled one way, but if you poked him on the other side it had the opposite effect. They had almost forgotten why they kidnapped him.

Jasper pulled one of the man's braces very tight and let it go. The **thwack** was loud and his eye rolled like a ball on a roulette wheel. "Why are you digging?" snapped Jasper.

The man known as Swivelling Simon began to talk.

*

The rest of the road gang had looked everywhere.

Well, everywhere where they could all fit at the same time. They were finding this Valley a bit intimidating, so they stuck together.

Back at the tent Buster was convinced that a crow perched on top was listening to them, so he swiped it away with his shovel.

The crow leapt and the shovel sliced a rend in the striped material. The crow landed and Buster struck again. Eventually the crow took the hint and flew away, leaving Buster triumphant amid a pile of red and white confetti.

"Oh great," said the drains Inspector, "Now we don't have a tent either."

*

Marvin settled upon a unique solution to his road gang interrogations.

He stood outside with the window open and screamed at them from there. He could have made them stand outside to relieve 'cubicle city' of the problem, but they could find their own solution.

"You need another what?" he yelled.

The men shuffled as the drains Inspector mumbled, "Everything."

Simon joined them on the walk back just after they had discovered that the van had gone as well, and now he spoke up in his own defence. "I'll have you know I was tortured," he said ripping open his shirt to show a single red mark. "I kept to the code too. I didn't tell them anything."

Buster muttered, "You told them about the hole."

Louie said, "You told them we were digging for drains."

The drains Inspector added grimly, "And you told them where the key for the van was."

Marvin almost exploded, "It sounds like you told them *everything!* Caved in to the demands of a bunch of juvenile shrubbery, *Snivelling* Simon, more like! It's a good job you didn't know why we are digging, isn't it?" Marvin checked himself. All eyes were on him. He seemed to have dug his own hole now!

*

Jasper sat at Cuthbert's table feeding the crow bits of bacon as he gave his report to the assembly, "He didn't know anything. They just think they're digging drains."

Ronald growled, "Did you press him hard enough, what limbs has he left?"

Jasper looked at Ronald and snapped, "We learnt our tricks from that Marquis chap's wife, Sadie. They always crack. We got *him* to talk didn't we?"

Jasper nodded towards Percy recalling an earlier embarrassment.

Ronald sneered, "Ooh that's hard getting Percy to talk; try shutting him up, that's the challenge."

Percy kept out of it. He was upset at seeing Jasper with the crow. He was missing his parrot. Percy sniffed and the attention reluctantly turned to him.

"Bad memories of my interrogation?" sneered Ronald.

"Just thinking about some of my lost pets," he said.

"Checked in your wellies?" asked Cuthbert, still smarting from the lion's cage fiasco.

Percy glared, "I tried to buy an exotic pet once, but they kept sending me an empty box. It was really disappointing."

49

"Did you complain?" asked Henry, showing his concern.

"Oh yes," said Percy. "Seven times, but they kept replacing it with another empty box. I got sick of throwing them out."

As the roomful of people tried to absorb this, Henry suddenly asked, "Just a minute Percy, what was this exotic pet you ordered?"

Percy sighed again. "A chameleon."

Henry sat back in his chair. "A chameleon, as in the creature capable of changing its camouflage to suit its surroundings?"

"Yep, that's the one" said Percy sadly.

"You twerp!" said Henry, "You threw away seven chameleons, not seven empty boxes."

"Oh!" said Percy, sheepishly heading for the door and tripping slightly. *Must be another chameleon*, he thought.

*

The women were heading home full of chatter, and tired.

It was really rewarding looking after the animals. All of their children had flown the nest and their husbands rather expected to be looked after; whereas the animals appreciated everything and were much more cuddly. They didn't leave socks lying about everywhere for a start.

As the women approached the site the road gang had chosen, Margery had a thought. "Geraldine, has anyone checked the site for archaeological significance?"

Geraldine stopped. "What a wonderful thought. We really should have an exploratory dig before any major roadworks start."

They stood gazing around them as they said their goodbyes, and Elspeth happened to say aloud, "Your pub sign could do with a good dust, Margery."

Margery glanced at the suspended sign and gasped. Then she was gone! *Well*, thought Elspeth, ***She's*** *very touchy lately, must be her age.*

50

Chapter 14

Jasper and the crow had left, and Ronald gave up baiting Percy.

Henry and the Captain were arguing over some forgotten battle involving some chap that no-one remembered, and Cuthbert had refilled the kettle with de-scaler, boiled it, and put it in a cup ready to throw away.

Marjorie burst in from another room, panting for breath and with a quick, "Oh, thanks Cuthbert," she grabbed the cup and downed its contents. Rapidly turning purple, she then dashed out the front door.

"Was it Margery?" asked the Captain. Henry scratched his ear, saying, "No, it would have been a Greek name, they were fighting the Persians at the time."

*

Marvin had insisted upon an open air meeting. He sat on a bench on one side of a path, and the road gang sat on another at the other side.

Both sides of the meeting eyed the other with suspicion. Marvin gave in. He needed these men. His anonymous caller was not pleased by the delays and wanted results. Also the accounts committee seemed to have woken up to the fact that tools cost money. "All right," he began. "I have been informed that there is a large amount of treasure buried under the road, just where you are about to dig. It is supposed to be the inheritance of a member of the Valley, but it can't be stealing if he doesn't know anything about it, can it?"

The road gang exchanged glances, but remained silent.

Marvin pressed on, "Obviously, if we became partners, the proceeds would be split between us all."

The drains Inspector leaned forward. "If they don't know about it, why are they trying to stop us?"

Marvin thought for a moment. "I don't think they know, but they would try to stop anything. This is the Valley after all."

The meeting gradually hammered out an agreement. The drains Inspector leaned forward again, "So, for a generous percentage, we dig up and transport the treasure. Do you want my men to report to you in your office every day?"

Marvin blanched, "I'll give you a bigger percentage if they don't."

*

Margery spluttered her way back into the kitchen, out of breath and spitting iron-hard shrapnel. "Lion!" she spluttered, "Seen Lion!"

The men assumed the lion had escaped and promptly pushed the table up against the door before barring all the windows.

Margery waited patiently to get her breath back before shouting. "Not that lion you fools, the one on the pub sign."

Henry looked at her blankly, "What pub sign dear, ours?"

Margery spluttered a reply, "Of course it's ours, there's only one pub and it's only got one sign, and we own both of them."

The Captain said, "So now there are two of them?"

Margery produced the look which had kept the twins tamed indoors for years.

The men sat down quickly.

"The Mandrake Arms," she began. The men nodded, just in case that's what she expected. "It comprises of a shield flanked by two creatures holding a crown above it."

"What's the other one?" asked Percy.

What other one?" she asked in a daze.

Cuthbert said, "It's a witch."

Everyone said, "Ooh."

Margery said, "No, it flaming well isn't."

Percy and Cuthbert echoed, "Yes, it flaming well is."

Percy got carried away and shouted, "She's behind you."

Cuthbert had never seen Margery this close before. But then she had never had her hands around his throat before either! "What are you going on about?" she said shaking him back and forth.

Cuthbert stared both death and Margery in the face, until she let him go and stood with her hands on her hips before him.

"Well," coughed Cuthbert, "When mum took me through the village in my pram, she always said, *Those are the arms of Narnia. There's the lion, there's the witch, and they are opening the wardrobe.*" He rubbed his neck as Margery slumped into a chair.

She thought, *Somehow, some folks have had a bigger dose of this Valley than I have.*

52

*

The road gang sat in their cabin.

The smog had built up nicely and Buster had toasted his jam sandwiches, so there was a sweet tang in the air. "What do we think lads, do we trust this bloke?" The drains Inspector already knew the answer as he asked the question.

These men were the 'Storm Troopers' of the Local authority. They got all the dirty jobs! They always went in first. Oddly enough, they all sat gazing at their drinks and no-one said anything.

"Buster?" he asked. Buster struggled to put *anything* into words and as this was a 'biggie,' he settled for a shrug.

"Simon?" Simon simply rubbed his friction burnt chest and contributed another shrug.

"Louie?"

Louie came out with, "Hurr, can't run as well as I used to."

The drains Inspector sat down heavily. "I don't believe it; the hardest men in the Authority turning down adventure, money and women."

Simon looked up, "The women won't be up to much if they're buried with the treasure."

The drains Inspector snarled, "Well, I rather thought you might find some new ones, once you had some money."

Mistake!

Louie was horrified, "New one! There's nothing wrong with my old one."

Buster was appalled, "How can I replace my old mum?"

Simon asked, "*You can buy them?*"

The drains Inspector slumped. "Well that's it then, the end of the 'Untouchables' - the men avoided by all. No-one could penetrate either our mystique or our cabin, and now it's all over." He rose wearily to his feet and opened the door. The smog made no attempt to leave with him. Just as he was slowly closing the door he played his trump card, "I'll nip round to the street sweepers then, shall I?"

He smiled at the sound of three chairs being simultaneously knocked backwards.

*

53

Margery had everyone's attention, mostly through terror, as she pointed out that the sign may be a *sign*!

Percy opened his mouth, saw Margery looking at him and didn't know what to do next, so shut it again.

Henry boldly asked, "But what difference does it make, dear? They are digging it up anyway."

Margery sighed and everyone moved away from Henry. "It means, my dear," said through gritted teeth, "That someone knows that there *is* something buried down there." The room went quiet. "Any questions?" asked Marjorie sarcastically.

The men simply couldn't resist it. "What's for dinner?", "Who won the three-thirty?", and "How much wood can a woodchuck chuck?" Then they ran. Unfortunately, the door was still blocked by the table!

Marjorie surveyed the captive species and asked, "Any *last* questions?"

Cuthbert meekly raised a hand, "How did you get in the house *this* time?"

*

The road gang were nearly set up again.

New kettle on new stove, surrounded by new tools, and all safely inside a new tent parked over old marks.

The drains Inspector stood to give his 'Eve of excavation' speech and the men stood to attention.

"Excuse me," said Geraldine sweetly. She entered the tent, placed a plastic bucket on the floor and knelt down.

"What are you doing?" asked the drains Inspector.

Geraldine snapped a rubber glove into place on her hand and picked out a soft bristle brush, "Just beginning a preliminary archaeological survey before we begin the main dig." Another glove snapped into place and Geraldine bent to her task, lightly brushing the surface of the road.

The men gawped as Geraldine swept and photographed, swept and photographed. She then began constructing a grid over the area covered by the council markings.

"How long will this take?" the drains Inspector eventually asked.

Geraldine looked up, "Oh, months I would think, and that would be a sloppy job. I happen to be a perfectionist." She carried on sweeping the same area again as if forgotting she had already done it.

The drains Inspector led his men outside. "This is a tricky one; if she finds something the job could be held up for years." He stroked his chin. "Simon, have you got the coins?"

Simon rummaged in his overalls and produced several misshapen lumps of metal.

The drains Inspector went back into the tent and coughed politely, "Excuse me miss. The lads found these over there, perhaps you are in the wrong place?"

Geraldine held the coins against her rubber hand and sighed. *My*, she thought, *That was a good try. If I was a rookie I would be over there right now*. Slipping them into her pocket she gushed, "Oh thank you so much, I'll put those on file and we can dig there next."

The drains Inspector slouched back to his men. "Back to the cabin lads, this is one for the higher-ups to sort out."

*

Henry, the Captain, Cuthbert, and Percy were getting back to normal after Margery left, her enthusiasm had been exhausting.

First she speculated the sign showed that the treasure *was* in the road after all; then she decided that the sign may mean that the treasure was *under* the sign and they may have to dig it up. But as she followed that point through she decided that the treasure may be under the Mandrake Arms itself. *Could the cellars be dug up?* she asked.

Henry gasped in alarm. "Darling, darling," he said to interrupt her. "We've already lost Mandrake Hall; the pub is all we have left."

Margery reminded him acidly, "*You* lost Mandrake Hall, *darling.*" After stirring up such volatile memories, she left!

Henry and the Captain agreed that the best strategy was to play 'a waiting game' and see what turned up.

Percy asked how anyone could make a game out of waiting.

The Captain snorted, but seemed at a loss to explain.

Henry tried. "It's like a game of chess Percy. Stay close to your own side of the board until you can see the other person's plan, then move to block and counter-attack."

Percy said, "Why not ask him?"

Henry leaned back, "Ask who?"

55

Percy flapped his hand, "The other chap."

The Captain joined in, "Which other chap?"

Percy tipped his cap back and eyed them both. "I've seen folk playing chess," he said. "They sit there for hours instead of just asking the other chap what he's going to do and getting on with it."

Henry gaped. The Captain spluttered. This was sacrilege! Henry had whiled away the hours all over the world. Race or country had been no barrier; he had played friend and foe alike. *Chess was an international language, like Latin*, he thought.

The Captain began to explain, "It's like a battle Percy. The lines are drawn up, both sides are evenly matched and they all follow the same rules."

Percy interrupted, "So it's not like a battle then?"

The Captain spluttered.

Henry took over. "It's an idealised battle, Percy. The deciding factor is in the way it's played." Henry paused and looked from Percy to Cuthbert and back again. "Do either of you know how to play?"

Both men said, "Oh yes, of course," whilst shaking their heads for 'not really'.

Now, Henry knew that Cuthbert had a chess set standing on a table in the other room. Elspeth was forever dusting it when she visited and the Captain always spent ages putting all the pieces back in the right place.

The board was set up between Henry and Percy.

Henry explained, "These little chaps are pawns, they are the foot soldiers and are valued the least."

Ronald entered the kitchen and sat down quietly. He knew entertainment when he saw it.

Henry lifted the tallest piece, "This is the King. He must be protected at all costs. If he is lost, the game is over." He picked up the next tallest. "This is the Queen, the most powerful piece on the board. This is the Bishop, he only moves diagonally …"

Everyone nodded as if they had shared a common experience.

"…The figure of a horse is called a knight and it is the only piece able to jump over the others. Then we have the castle; slow and ponderous, but perfect for hiding behind." Henry sat back and eyed Percy. "Have you got that?

Percy rubbed his chin. "The little bald chaps at the front are pawns, the King is useless, the Queen really runs the show. Castles are

56

solid, horses can jump, and the bishop has a disability!" Percy was intrigued. "Let's go!"

Henry was a good and patient teacher, but the first game was annihilation. Percy had interrupted with a few questions, *Can you do that?*, *Is that allowed?* and *Why are the King and Queen so alike? Shouldn't one of them be wearing a frock?* He only sulked once when Henry would not accept that Percy had installed lasers at the top of his castles and could zap anything in range.

Several games passed in this way and Cuthbert, Ronald, and the Captain, wandered away or dozed in an armchair.

A cry of *Check friend* caught everybody's attention, it was Percy's voice! The kitchen filled with people again as a stunned Henry gaped first at the board and then at Percy.

Henry stammered, "Ch, ch, check friend?"

Ronald slapped Percy on the shoulder and yelled, "It's *mate*, mate. Checkmate, well done!"

Henry's expression was becoming grim. They had played all night and he had lost the last seven games. His eyes felt as if they were hanging out of his head and his brain was wearing a belt pulled far too tight!

Percy was still jumping up and down as if he had just won a tractor competition. Henry managed to congratulate Percy and humbly asked Ronald and the Captain to take him home.

Cuthbert served the winner with a steaming mug of whatever was left in the pot and sat opposite him across the board. Watching Percy bubble with excitement, Cuthbert waited for a while and then asked. "All right, how did you do it?"

Percy sat forward. "These military types are all the same, old battles, Generals who should have been locked away years ago. I simply changed the references to something I understood." He grinned.

"Go on," encouraged Cuthbert.

Percy shuffled. "Well, I thought of my pawns as locusts, if I sent them in first they would chew up his defences. The King had to be protected at all times, so I had him clocked as a big daft dahlia. The Queen was a wild rose, beautiful but don't get too close! The knights are vine-weevil beetles, they can jump, they take a bite out of everything, and they're hard to kill. I saw the bishops as ivy, you think you know where they are, but they suddenly shoot off in a different direction, the 'Holy and the Ivy' if you like. The castle was simply a turnip. Very hard to shift is a turnip, especially after you've eaten one."

Cuthbert was impressed. "The strategy?"

"Simple," smiled Percy. "Send a squadron of locusts in to chew up his pawns, leave the daft dahlia where it is. Send the queen out to one side to attract all the admiring glances and while they're distracted let the vine weevil's jump in amongst them. Leave the ivy where reinforcements can trip over it and roll a turnip straight down the middle. And that's check-friend, mate!"

*

Henry was in shock! He had always given a good account of himself at chess. He used to play one of the Russian mercenaries in exchange for inside news.

Margery fussed around him and Ronald asked suspiciously, "Do you think the little twerp already knew how to play?"

Henry considered this. "No," he was adamant. "It was as if he analysed it, peeled away anything he didn't need and got straight to the heart-wood. I could almost believe that he got hold of the rule book, read through and 'dead-headed' it." He shook his head in wonder and Margery stroked his hand.

"Thought any more about digging up the cellar?" she asked.

Chapter 15

The elephant decided that it was a funny old world.

If he wandered off, people came after him. But, if he walked towards them, they ran away! He was fascinated by the way people lived. They considered themselves safe inside these buildings and yet whenever he leant on anything, it collapsed!

The first time he had wandered since coming here was quite worrying. He'd plodded into the village and approached a black and white creature standing by the road. Thinking he had found a badger he performed a friendly shuffle for it, but got no reaction. Picking it up with his trunk and turning it around caused pandemonium. Apparently, it could only see behind it!

Blind Pugh panicked in one direction and the elephant fled in the other. Ending up on the top of a hill watching two strange chaps jump over a cliff in front of him hadn't helped either.

The next time was when he fancied a nice bit of bush. The first one moved! So did the second one, so he started putting one foot on them to hold them steady. He had never heard a bush make that sound before. When all the bushes ganged up on him he ran through the village and came out the other end wearing a striped shirt!

Now, though, he seemed to have everything sorted. The crow had started riding on his head, steering him by pecking to the left if that was the best way, and to the right if needed. It was really useful because the crow had a better view from up there, it would be a good place for a crow's nest.

They discussed patenting the idea and calling it Tap-Nav; it could be fitted to elephants worldwide so that holidays to the Serengeti could become a community thing.

Also, it gave the elephant a friend. The lion never went out, the hippo was only interested in pool, and the giraffe thought it was above everybody!

The only downside was the way the crow's claws tickled when he moved around. Unless it was the crow-flies, which he'd heard about. Another slight worry was introduced by a lady friend, she thought that the idea was good in principle, but it might have an ageing effect. All her friends desperately tried to avoid *crows feet*!

59

Chapter 16

Marvin studied the letter before him. It bore the heading of the Valley museum and it was signed by the curator, but it smelled of collusion.

Actually, when the road gang wasn't around, Marvin found that his sense of smell had heightened. "Archaeological dig!" he snorted. He had just screwed the letter up and launched it, when his intercom crackled. It sounded like *Local supporter wants to be you!*

Marvin enjoyed these meetings, some local benefactor wanting to praise his efforts and buy him something, if he could just slightly influence something. "Alright," he barked, and started to rearrange his blotter and pencil. He looked up as Avril entered his office with a notebook already open.

"Good morning, thank you for seeing me," she chirped.

Marvin spluttered, "I didn't know it was you."

Avril smiled, "I distinctly heard the receptionist say, *Local reporter wants to see you*; I was standing right there."

Marvin stabbed the intercom button, "You know I never see the press," he snapped.

The hurt reply crackled back, "She never said she was wearing a vest."

Avril took a seat as Marvin fumed. He could sense conspiracy and there was that smell of collusion again.

Smiling sweetly Avril asked, "I hear that you have kindly suspended intensive road works in the village to allow an archaeological dig. Do you think they will find anything interesting?"

The meeting lasted forever. Marvin was forced to record his support for the venture and Avril thanked him on behalf of 'all collectors of artefacts everywhere'. Standing to take her leave she glanced into the waste-bin where a crumpled museum heading could be seen. "Cool filing system," she said; then left.

Marvin seethed. He had been played, he had been duped, there it was again, that smell.

Suddenly there was another smell and it certainly wasn't collusion. Resigned, he opened a window and called, "Come in!"

The Inspector of drains sat where Avril had been. Marvin wished it was the other way around. The road gang stood around the outer walls.

The drains Inspector said, "We hear that this museum woman has pulled a fast one over you."

"Made you look a right mug," said Simon.

"Made you look small," added Louie.

Buster hadn't been briefed, so he kept quiet.

"Get to the point," snapped Marvin, trying to strangle the pencil he had named 'Avril'.

The drains Inspector leant forward and his own personal miasma came with him. "Tunnels," he said.

"Tunnels?" asked Marvin, trying to talk through his nose.

"You said this village is riddled with tunnels. We can work from underneath."

Marvin relaxed. *Gain some credibility, quickly*, he thought. "You read my memo then?"

The gang looked blank, "Memo?" No-one ever came close enough to the cabin to deliver anything.

"Oh yes," bluffed Marvin, "It was all in there; it must still be in the office system, somewhere."

Buster said, "Either that, or it is a cynical attempt to emulate the decisions of a greater mind."

Even the smell retreated at this intrusion of mass incredulity.

Buster looked up from the leaflet he was reading, embarrassed that he had spoken aloud. "Sorry, I am studying to be a road sweeper."

"Do we really have to meet in a graveyard at night?" the drains Inspector hissed.

Marvin shushed him. "This isn't a normal community. Don't expect to see normal things at normal hours." Then he added, "This is where the old reservoir was. I know for a fact that it is linked by tunnels. So that's where we will start."

Since the cemetery had been re-laid it was simple to find anything, so Marvin was able to lead them straight to the entrance.

"No lights until we get down there," whispered the drains Inspector to the team huddled behind him.

Chapter 17

Percy sat down by the hooded figure on the edge of the reservoir. "Watcha doin' Whistle?" he asked the shadowy figure.

Whistle turned slightly to identify Percy by his voice and the fact that only three of them were daft enough to come up here at night. Cuthbert would have sneaked up on him like an elephant in cornflakes, so it must be the other one.

"Night fishing, Percy," came the reply. "Whistle see a lot of interest in this hobby soon."

Percy dangled his legs over the edge, and asked, "Do all these tunnels link up then? How long would it take a fish to come right back round to you if you missed it?"

Whistle gasped, "That's the whole essence of it, Percy. All the others think I'm barmy, but you have got it in one. Try to think of it as an extra dimension to fishing. Try to imagine a fish lying on its side, easy to scoop up. That's one dimensional, that is." The hood turned further towards Percy as he continued. "If you imagine the same fish swimming in the deep water where it can go up, down, sideways or even diagonally, it would have three dimensions. Now, most fishermen are satisfied with that. But Whistle try for something even deeper." He paused dramatically, "Whistle have all that to cope with and then factor in the tunnels. Whistle be trying to catch them, when we don't even know where they are. Any fool can fish for things when he knows where they are! I have sat here quietly for years, perfecting four-dimensional fishing!"

Percy swung his little legs and thought, *Yes, and if you factor in some water mate, you've just entered the fifth dimension!* Percy said goodbye and lowered himself into the dry reservoir. He fancied a walk home through the tunnels and set off downhill.

Whistle shook his head in disgust. *Waste of a bright lad*, he thought, *He'll get soaked.*

Percy didn't really need lights when he went through the tunnels; he just trailed his fingers along the walls on one side. Sometimes it was brick and sometimes stone, depending on the age of the system he was in. If the wall stopped and his hand was in mid-air, then he had reached a junction. Decisions like that made it fun.

Tonight there was a murmur in the tunnels, and a strange smell! Percy stopped to listen. Hurrying to a junction he spotted bright lights and shadows dancing off the walls. *Ooh!* thought Percy, and sped up.

Buster was bringing up the rear. His instructions were clear. "Keep your torch on the man in front. Don't lose sight of him for a second." Buster was quietly repeating this to himself as he walked.

"Nice and cool down here, isn't it?" asked a voice behind him.

"I've been in worse," said Buster, watching the man in front carefully.

Percy tried not to breathe in too deeply, "I can believe that."

Buster kept the circle of his torch beam centred on the back of the man in front.

Percy asked, "Vampire hunting, are you?"

Buster's torch leapt all over the place until it was firmly back on the man in front. He was suddenly conscious of the faint *slap, slap* of Percy's wellies behind him. Just as he was considering looking behind him, the voice came again.

"Went vampire hunting on my own, once; unsociable critters they were too."

Buster sneered, "No such thing."

Percy replied, "That's the trouble! People watch a film or two and think they know what they're looking for." *Slap, slap.*

"What do you mean?" asked Buster.

Percy said, "Well, vampires watch films as well you know. We've given them all our secrets now. They know where we look and what we look for. So, they keep out of the way and use different methods now." *Slap, slap.*

Buster's torch wandered briefly before settling down again. "What sort of methods?" asked Buster suspiciously.

Percy continued, "Well, not many people go out alone at night anymore do they? So, a chap in a cloak with spiky teeth is going to stand out a bit. No, the trick is to get into a position of authority and *make* people go out into the dark."

Buster latched on to a word he recognised, "What sort of authority?"

Slap, slap. Percy said, "Oh, any sort, minor authority, government authority, even *local authority*!" *Slap, slap.*

Buster stumbled and his torch lit the curved roof of the tunnel, those were *two* words he recognised!

63

"Keep up Buster," hissed the man in front. The torch beam settled again.

Buster trembled when he asked, "How would he do that?"

Slap, slap. Percy smirked, composing himself. "Well, I suppose he would simply dream up an excuse to lead someone into a dark secluded place where no-one would hear the screams." *Slap, slap.* "Then he would stop for supper!"

Buster was starting to get the picture! His trembling became so bad that the torch was flickering; he'd shaken the bulb loose. He tried one last thing to hang onto reality. "We've talked for hours in the cabin and you've never said anything. Why's that?"

Slap, slap. Percy lowered his voice and intoned, "Because we've never met," and he turned left!

Buster swung round sharply with his torch flickering wildly, there was no-one there! Buster let out a yell which tripped everyone's sanity switch and the whole procession went screaming downhill, skidding to a halt on the concrete lake.

The drains Inspector took deep breaths; dusted himself down and went to help Louie and Simon restrain Buster. For some reason he was trying to push a wooden fence post through Marvin's chest!

Chapter 18

When Percy entered Cuthbert's kitchen and relayed his adventure, it caused a real panic; no-one thought of using the tunnels.

It was obvious when they thought about it. Anyone digging the road up to bury something big would attract attention. But, if the tunnels already led to an underground room the job was half done!

Everyone began to draw their own versions of the tunnel system. Each of them had been down there for one reason or another at some time. After a quiet period of licking pencils and sticking out tongues, the drawings were compared. Not one drawing agreed with another and none of the tunnels went near to the village street anyway!

Ronald suggested a full survey, and the Captain and Henry agreed. Cuthbert pointed out that the local authority may already have plans for the whole valley, and Percy had nodded off!

*

Everyone slept over at Cuthbert's until the next morning. Henry put a spell on the cooking range and produced a wonderful breakfast for everyone.

Percy woke up and pieced together the plan of a survey. He yawned and asked, "What will you do if they are already down there?"

No-one had thought of that. A huge discussion ensued with Ronald suggesting assault troops and flame throwers.

Nothing really obvious appealed to everybody, until Percy woke up again. Listening for a moment to get the gist of things, he snorted, "It would take a hippo to clear those tunnels," and nodded off again.

"How does he do it?" asked Henry.

Cuthbert shrugged, "Natural talent."

Ronald muttered, "Only thing natural about him then."

*

The hippo expected very little from life. Cool water, cool mud, and a daily diet of whatever it was in those buckets people threw at him. Being born into captivity meant not needing to know the finer details.

He expected the sun to shine and those little birds to turn up on time to pick his teeth for him. What he didn't expect was a crowd of people to suddenly focus on him, whilst one of them drove an excavator at him! Being lifted into the air was a first too!

This would be how the giraffe saw the world if it had a brain behind its eyes!

The hippo had watched in amusement as the elephant was fastened to the excavator to get him up the hill. The elephant was a real enigma to the hippo. At one stage the hippo expected to turn into an elephant because it was the only big grey reference point he had, but the ears had stubbornly refused to budge and his cute stubby nose didn't lengthen. He just assumed that every species had a lesser cousin. That's why the elephant was pulling and he was riding!

At the top of the hill everyone stopped and gaped into an empty square hole. The hippo felt himself going down!

*

Margery went down the ancient stone steps into the cellar of the Mandrake Arms. How come Henry could play the role of landlord and 'mine host' so successfully, and yet always be missing when the barrels needed changing?

Turning the corner into the cellar, she stopped. Her hand went to her throat and she gasped. Bricks and plaster everywhere! How could she have doubted him? He had started digging up the cellar floor. Actually, she had to admit that it seemed to be the wall which had been attacked, but it was a start.

The hippo looked at Margery, and Margery looked at the hippo. As each of them possessed a brain from each end of the spectrum, it was a mutual decision to not acknowledge the presence of the other.

Margery went back upstairs and the hippo lumbered back into the tunnels.

Chapter 19

Marvin had gone home, seriously considering having Buster committed. The road gang sat in the cabin with the lights on very brightly.

Buster was pleading, "Someone must have heard the slapping."

"Someone needed slapping," muttered Simon.

Buster looked down into his lap, mumbling, "I know what I heard. Everything fitted. The voice said that our boss is a vampire."

The Inspector of drains had to take charge and rebuild morale. The trouble was that he actually found Marvin quite strange. The man didn't have a smell about him for a start. The Inspector of drains could recognise each man of his team in the dark inside a large pipe. For a man to not have a smell was, well … unnatural!

Louie pointed out that Marvin spent hours alone in his office and there wasn't a mirror anywhere in it either. Louie sat back pleased at this observation, until he glanced around the cabin and saw that they hadn't one either!

The Inspector of drains looked at Buster, "Didn't you get a look at this chap at all?

Buster said miserably, "No, I was watching the man in front like you told me to."

"But you were the last man," Simon pointed out.

Buster concurred, "Yes, I know, but voices in the dark are all part of this job, so I didn't think anything of it."

Everyone nodded at the wisdom of this statement. Louie spoke for them all. "The question is, do we trust this bloke and keep going down tunnels with him, or do we give this whole business a miss?"

Silence reigned as each man thought out his personal circumstances and needs.

'One-lung' Louie spoke first. "The money would come in handy. I could do with some breathing space."

Buster said, "If I get my promotion to the road sweepers, I'll have to buy a brush."

Swivelling Simon nodded and said, "I must admit I've got my eye on something."

The drains Inspector stood over his men, saying, "That's it then, we can always take precautions lads."

Buster asked, "What, garlic?"

The others recoiled immediately and echoed, "Can't stand the smell of the stuff!"

*

Henry, the Captain, Cuthbert, Ronald and Percy stood in the cellar of the Mandrake Arms. The hippo-shaped hole was quite tidy, but the bricks and plaster all over the previously immaculate floor was a disgrace.

Henry turned to Percy. "You and your bright ideas," he said with accusation.

Ronald slapped Percy on the shoulder, laughing, "No-one goes from hero to zero quite like you, Percy."

Percy just muttered and looked around to see if any barrels were leaking.

The Captain looked around at everyone and asked, "Do you think it's still in there? Have you seen it back at the farm, Cuthbert?"

Cuthbert shrugged, "They all still turn their backs on me. I can't tell one from another."

Visions of various shaped animal backsides flitted across various brains, but risking a peek into Cuthbert's psyche wasn't worth the risk, so they gave up.

The Captain edged into the hole and peered into the darkness. "This must be a whole new section for us, shall we explore?"

"Is it safe?" asked Henry.

The Captain leaned around the corner and stretched out his arm. "Bit damp in places," he said, exploring the hippo's nostril in the dark, then wiping his hand on the back of Percy's coat.

The hippo had never had his nose tickled before. He thought it was the way to wind kittens up and make them purr. The resulting sneeze, magnified by the tunnels, blew him backwards and further into the darkness.

The men in the cellar recoiled from the hole in the wall. "Sounds like a tunnel collapse further along," said Henry. "Could they be old mine workings, do you think?"

Percy whispered, "*Gold Mine!*" and everyone forgot to breathe.

68

*

Marvin stood outside his office on the grass and spoke to the road gang seated inside.

"Look," he said forcefully. "We are the local authority. No-one knows what we do; therefore no-one knows what we are capable of. We simply dig somewhere else and break into the nearest tunnel, then follow it in the right direction. If anyone asks questions, we have the authority."

Simon nodded, "And the striped tent!"

Buster said, "An abuse of authority is quite normal, but should only be used to further our aims."

Marvin peered into the office, "Are you reading again, Buster?"

Buster nodded, "The way to advancement is to verbally agree, but rebel in your heart."

Marvin had heard enough. Taking a deep breath he leaned into the office and snatched a pamphlet from Buster. Holding it at arm's length he flicked through the pages and asked, "Who the blazes is Red Ronnie?

Buster said, "I was given that when I applied for promotion. It is A-guide-to-advancement-within- the-proletarian-ranks-of-the-government-lackey-local-authority." Each word was stamped out with the precision of a lesson learned by constant repetition.

Marvin was appalled. "This is an Anti-government-subversive-document!" He said each word stamped out in the manner of those authorities about to be subverted.

Louie snorted, "Leave the lad be; he is simply activating his rights as enshrined in the charter, representing those below-stairs."

Simon contributed, "You don't get much further below stairs than this job either."

Marvin was alarmed. "You've read it too. And your speeches weren't full of hyphens either. Are you all at it?" He looked accusingly at the drains Inspector.

The man blushed slightly, drew himself up to his full height and said, "I have no truck with the commie-agitator type goings on, Sir. I am at one with the management, brother."

Now, this was almost perfect, if he hadn't added 'Brother' at the end he would have been free and clear!

Marvin dismissed them and waited for quite a while to clear the

69

air, composing a memo for an enquiry into Red Ronnie.

Chapter 20

The group were gathered. Ronald had his combat overalls on and every pocket was full. His torch could have signalled to the moon, if he had remembered to buy batteries.

Henry loaned him something more modest. There were two directions to choose from and neither of them went under the street.

A glimpse of a pair of small red eyes in one direction convinced Ronald to lead off in the other. Excitement mounted when they realised they were stumbling along a miniature railway track.

"Gold," whispered Percy.

Accompanied by the reassuring s*lap, slap* of Percy's wellies, the group moved ahead.

"Look!" said Ronald from the front. The group clustered around a discarded shovel and a rusty old garden fork.

"For riddling the ore," suggested Cuthbert.

"Don't move anything," said Henry urgently. "We can let Geraldine excavate it and it will be the Valley's secret until the gold runs out; the perfect disguise for us."

The wisdom of this appealed to them all, and they moved on. The air was fresh and quite cool. Percy knew a way to tell which way the wind was blowing, so he licked his finger and held it up. He then spent ten minutes furiously rubbing his tongue and spitting madly whilst he tried to remember where his finger had been, by then he had forgotten why he had done it in the first place.

Ronald gave a mysterious hand signal.

Henry had been a mason but his memory of the signals was a bit hazy, so everybody bumped into the back of each other as he wracked his brains for the right reply.

Ronald hissed, "It means *stop*! Henry, *stop.*"

Henry muttered, "Not in my lodge, it didn't."

There were noises coming from ahead and there seemed to be a room branching off to one side.

Ronald hissed, "Let's back up and get ready for an assault."

The Captain asked, "Are you sure someone will tell us before we're assaulted?"

Ronald snarled, "Not us you twit. *We* are doing the assaulting.

71

Now back up, back up."

Percy piped up from the back. "Er, slight problem there chaps."

"What is it now?"

"The tunnel's blocked," said Percy.

"Landslide?" asked the Captain.

Percy poked the obstruction.

The hippo bellowed in outrage and the 'Assault team' fled into the side room, slamming the door behind them.

"Come in, why don't you?" said Jasper sarcastically. He was sitting at a desk in front of a bank of flickering monitors.

The visitors gaped.

"That's the village street," said the Captain.

"That's the village Post Office," said Henry, as the screen was white due to powder on the lens.

Jasper sighed. "Real pain that one. We have to keep going in to clean it, but when Mrs Biggle spots us she tries to call the Police!"

Percy stared hard at one screen, and said, "Is that my shed?"

Cuthbert asked, "What are you doing in our gold mine?"

Jasper laughed, "*Your goldmine*? The twins set this up years ago. You didn't even know it was here. Besides, what makes you think there's gold?"

Even Cuthbert had allowed gold-fever to seep into his blood and was not going to be fooled. "The rails and the shovel and riddling fork," he declared.

Jasper regarded the adults with the look children reserve for adults all over the world. "The rails," he began, "Date back to when the Mandrake arms had real ale delivered in huge wooden casks. Not the gnat-sweat they serve now. They were rolled down a long ramp and then along the rails into the cellar."

Cuthbert persisted, "What about the shovel and fork?"

Jasper grinned at Percy, "We nicked them off him, months ago, and he never noticed. Some gardener!"

Percy scowled, "I'd worn them out actually."

"Anyway," said Jasper. "Why are you lot standing here?"

"There's a hippo outside the door," said Percy expecting the team to back him up. No-one looked at him or acknowledged his explanation.

"Of course there is, Percy. Of course there is," said Jasper wearily. Operating a toggle switch in front of him Jasper scanned the tunnels.

72

They were empty. "I suppose it's looking for the 'elephant in the room' as well, eh, Percy?" Jasper asked sarcastically.

Back in the tunnels Percy rounded on his companions. "Why didn't you back me up?"

Henry said, "Who would have believed that?"

Percy shouted, "We did! We ran fast enough."

Ronald cleared his throat and rambled on about 'strategic positioning' and 'tactical necessity' until Percy's wellies could be heard slapping away from them down the dark corridor.

Cuthbert scratched his head.

Henry noticed and asked, "Will he be alright?"

Cuthbert thought for a minute before replying, "Oh yes, it's the hippo I'm worried about."

Chapter 21

Marvin had received disquieting news.

The Mayor's office revealed that Red Ronnie had been active for some time now and was becoming a problem. There was an undercurrent of refuse men who thought they were too good to handle dustbins, Rat Catchers who thought the rats should be encouraged to surrender themselves, only during office hours, and litter pickers who insisted upon laying siege to supermarkets to stop the stuff at source.

Marvin saw an opportunity! He offered himself as a 'Mole', but the woman in the Mayor's office assured him that *all* the rodent officers were playing up. Marvin changed tack and offered to 'infiltrate the inner echelons'.

The woman in the Mayor's office was certain they had an outside firm to do that. Marvin then offered to become 'Deep Throat' and the woman in the Mayor's office slammed the phone down on him.

Marvin looked at the purring receiver in his hand. *Hmm, very obstructive!* he thought, *Perhaps **she** was Red Ronnie.* Marvin thought it may be time to start a list of possible Red Ronnie's. *Where could he start his list?*

*

Percy slapped on down the tunnels. He seemed to achieve more on his own anyway. That bunch managed to confuse each other, even by checking the roster before they set out. Trailing his hand against the wall, he merrily slapped on alone.

The hippo was bouncing along nicely too, humming as he went. Out on the African plains his relatives had never really thought about acoustics. But down here he was surprised to discover that he was an accomplished baritone. The march from Carmen was really good company!

*

Ronald, the Captain, and Henry, had talked Cuthbert into giving them a hand to clear up the mess in the cellar.

As they stacked bricks and swept the floors, Cuthbert asked, "What was it really like to have fought in real wars?"

He had read about World War I where almost everyone was killed, and it played on his mind. As an undertaker, the logistics probably kept him awake at night.

"It must have been awful when the whistle blew and everyone went over the top," he said.

The Captain replied, "Is that what that meant? I thought it was breakfast. I wondered where the queue's had gone."

*

Marvin remembered that one tunnel came out at the concrete lake. He assembled his team, checked their torches, and led off into echoing darkness.

Buster still brought up the rear and had been warned to 'Watch the man in front and as you're the last man, watch for the chap behind as well!' After reaching first a junction and then a fork in the tunnels, Buster began to recognise the *slap, slap* behind him.

"Still vampire hunting, are we?" asked Percy conversationally.

"Don't be silly! You got me into trouble, you did. My boss was very annoyed."

Percy said, "Well he would be, wouldn't he? Out of the whole team you were the only one to spot him." *Slap, slap.*

Buster liked that, "Yeah, well he's convinced me that he isn't one now, so go away."

Percy rejoined with, "Well, he wouldn't be one now, would he? I bet he's a shape-shifter. He'll be something else now." *Slap, slap.*

Buster pondered. "What's a shirt-lifter?"

Percy corrected him, "No, shape-shifter. I bet he's a zombie now. Did he meet you in the graveyard again?" *Slap, slap.*

Buster's torch wavered slightly. Then he remembered. "No, we met at this big solid pond this time."

Percy paused for his thoughts to catch up. Then he said, "Yes, just as I thought. That's where they were all buried under concrete." *Slap, slap.*

Buster stumbled, "You mean he escaped?"

Percy's tone was grave, "Not only that, he may have brought others with him." *Slap, slap.*

75

They walked in silence for a while after Marvin shouted, "Is someone talking back there?"

"Not me," said Louie.

"Not me," said Simon.

"Er, not me," said Buster.

"Me neither," said Percy.

After a few more steps with nothing other than *slap, slap,* Buster asked, "What can I do?"

"Surround him with mirrors," said Percy promptly. "Hold them up all around him and you will see a different face in each one. That will panic him into revealing who he really is." *Slap, slap.*

Buster nodded, "That's clever, that is. Thanks mister."

Percy had begun to feel a hot breath on the back of his neck, so he took the pamphlet sticking out of Buster's pocket and turned left.

Buster felt relieved. He was one of life's followers. He needed an instruction or a plan. Now he had a plan. Behind him someone began to hum. Buster didn't know what it was, but joined in anyway.

Gradually the man in front began to join in as well; and there began quite a tuneful rendition of Bizet's *Carmen.*

Marvin at the front smiled to himself. He was beginning to feel part of this team, so he allowed himself to hum along too.

Before long Marvin began to hear the *clunk* of bricks being stacked and the mutter of conversation. Holding up his hand, he said, "Shush men."

The humming went on and Marvin tried, "Yes, alright lads, I like Carmen as much as anyone, but there's a time and a place, now, shush."

The humming had become 'dum-dum-dum-dum' now, and was getting louder as the men were swept away by repetition.

Marvin turned.

The drains Inspector blushed furiously when Marvin shushed him. It wasn't often that he let his official status slip.

Marvin shone his torch at Louie and said, "Shush," before letting him pass. It worked.

Shining his torch at Simon, Marvin again said, "Shush," and let him pass.

Buster stopped reluctantly and seemed to give him a strange look as he passed.

The hippo had been well into his stride; humming away, head

swinging to the rhythm, when suddenly he was blinded by a light and 'shushed'. He opened his enormous mouth and snapped it shut, covering the offending light. This merely channelled the beam straight back out of his nostrils and into Marvin's face!

Screams mixed with bellow, and the team bomb-burst in all directions, down tunnels they hadn't known were there.

Marvin had voluntarily abandoned his torch, and was fleeing in complete darkness faster than he had ever run in the light. He came out behind a tree in the children's park.

Louie turned into the pub cellar and calmly inspected the damage saying, "Hurr, hurr, good work chaps, hurr," before fleeing upstairs.

Buster somehow ended up tip-toeing across the concrete lake, trying not to disturb the residents.

Swivelling Simon came up in a badly finished grave, holding someone else's hand, and Percy was back at the farm acquainting himself with Red Ronnie.

The rest were re-stacking the bricks again.

Chapter 22

"Look at this, Cuthbert," said Percy as his friend entered the kitchen. "It looks as if Marvin has got an agitator."

"Haven't we all," muttered Cuthbert, smiling at the hand-pump in an attempt to get it to wash the brick dust off. It just coughed politely back at him.

Cuthbert scanned the pamphlet and asked, "Where did you get this?"

Percy shrugged, "In the tunnels. How do you become a member of the proletariat? Is it subscription only?"

Cuthbert sat down, saying, "We should show this to Henry. He might have some ideas."

*

The road gang met up back at the local authority, just as Cubicle-city was getting ready to go home.

Anonymous heads were appearing above partitions and women were applying makeup for the journey home, in case Mister Right was waiting for a bus outside.

Buster loomed over several cubicles, overpowered the occupants with an odour which definitely wouldn't fit into a funny shaped bottle, and ushered the team into Marvin's office.

The other three simply looked at him as he handed them each a mirror and told them to stand at different points of the room holding them up.

The drains Inspector automatically opened the window. Marvin seemed to be a fresh air freak. Louie breathed on the mirror and steamed it up just to make sure that his one lung was still working. Simon swivelled his eye towards a list of names starting at the top of Marvin's wall. Buster waited patiently.

Marvin was fully occupied by his thoughts as he opened his office door. The smell took him completely by surprise and he doubled over at the shock.

"Now," shouted Buster, and they all moved inwards. The mirrors were reflecting way above Marvin and all they saw was each other!

"Arrgh! It's us!" cried Buster. "We're all zombies," and they fled in panic.

Marvin straightened up and allowed the air to clear. He really did quite enjoy being part of a clique, but some of these 'buddy-pranks' were beyond him.

*

Henry studied the pamphlet. "It seems that something is rotten in the state of Denmark," he said pompously.

Percy and Cuthbert exchanged glances. "Is that where it was printed?" asked Percy.

"It's a quotation," explained Henry. "Shakespeare," he added.

"Why did he write it in Denmark?" asked Cuthbert.

"Perhaps on holiday and preferred the food there," said Percy.

Henry snapped, "Hamlet!"

Cuthbert was indignant, "Long way to go for an omelette, Percy."

Percy grinned, "Food for thought though, Cuthbert."

Henry grimaced; pomposity didn't work in Cuthbert's kitchen. Even the water pump didn't work in Cuthbert's kitchen.

*

The road gang sat in silence for a while. The sudden inrush of fresh air had ruined the ambience of the cabin and the smog had to build up again.

The questions began. "What was all that about?"

"What's with the mirrors?"

"What was that in the tunnel?"

"Where did everybody go?" And, "Where's my pamphlet?"

As there were four of them and there had been five questions, somebody must have been talking to themselves.

They began to calm down. "The mirrors?" prompted the Inspector of drains.

Buster explained that; "The tunnel demon warned him that Marvin was a shape-shifter. He *had* been a vampire and was now a zombie, but had managed to become all of the road gang as well."

One lung Louie asked hesitantly, "Hurr, is he here now?"

Simon allowed his eye to swivel uncontrollably as he pointed out,

"If he is all of us, then there is only one person here and none of them is us!"

The Inspector of drains gulped. Sometimes it was better to ignore Simon before he started to make sense. "Did you *see* this tunnel demon this time, Buster?" he asked, more as a distraction than anything else.

Buster pondered. "No, but I always hear a slapping noise when he's around, and then it goes away when he does."

The drains Inspector looked around the table. The foggy atmosphere was beginning to blur the faces of his team. "Anyone else see or hear anything?" he asked.

"Only you running for your life and scaring the rest of us," said Louie accusingly.

The drains Inspector bristled, "Didn't any of you see that tunnel monster? It was only my self-sacrifice that saved you all."

Simon said, "So now we have a 'Tunnel demon' and a 'tunnel monster,' and *we* could be anybody."

Both Buster and the Inspector of drains snapped in unison, "Are you calling us liars?"

Simon pounced and his eye swivelled wildly, "Aha! So you are *us* now. I am still me and Louie's still him, so who is a zombie now then?" He sat back in triumph, fading slightly as the smog enveloped him.

The drains Inspector looked at Buster, and Buster looked back at him. Reality stayed outside the door.

Chapter 23

Margery was becoming obsessed. She was convinced that the lion symbol was the key to the mystery.

The men were making a complete hash of excavating the cellar, so she had called a meeting of the rest of the women.

Outlining her theory, Margery asked for ideas from the others.

Geraldine said, "There is a lot of symbolism in the Valley, ladies." Before nastily adding, "The men are pretty symbolic for a start." She reminded them that an earlier search for Shakespeare's plays had been encouraged by finding symbols of a quill in an inkwell. "At a time when the population wasn't able to read or write, this was an accepted way to pass on knowledge."

"Is that why all the eggs had a little lion on them then?" asked Mrs. Biggle.

Geraldine was in official lecture mode and was caught unawares. "Pardon?" she spluttered.

Elspeth said, "Ooh, no dear, that would have meant that the gold was in the hen house."

Margery joined in, "Or on the back of the milk float."

Belinda offered, "My family stopped having gold top off the milk float, too many calories you know."

"Same with butter dear," said Margery, "Most of us stopped having that as well."

"Good for bruises though!" Elspeth reminded them.

Geraldine could see all the lips moving and hear the buzz of conversation, but couldn't recognise anything from her degree course at all. "Quiet!" she yelled. The lips stopped moving. The buzz stopped buzzing. "Lions, ladies, where would we find lions?"

Mrs Biggle came over all melancholy. "When we were kids we used to ride the lions. We pretended to have races, until some miserable devil chased us off." Everyone assumed that she had gone off on a ramble as she carried on. "Fierce looking creatures they were, but we loved them."

Margery leaned over and patted her hand, "Loved what dear?"

Mrs Biggle's eyes widened. "Why the lions each side of the steps at Mandrake Hall, of course."

*

Margery burst into Cuthbert's kitchen. The men were embarrassed because she never caught them doing anything interesting.

"Oh, you've found the door this time have you?" said Cuthbert sarcastically.

Margery ignored him and concentrated on her husband. "It's under the steps at Mandrake Hall!"

Henry looked around the table. Everyone knew what she meant. They all remembered the stone lions at the Hall.

"But dear," said Henry, "The Hall has gone. That's where the cinema stands now."

Margery relaxed slightly. "I know all that, but where did the lions go?"

Nobody knew. Henry thought for a while.

It was Ronald who said, "That antiques bloke in the next valley bought them."

"Who, Hepplewhite?" asked Henry.

Ronald nodded, "Yep, I sold him the bell as well."

Martin Hepplewhite was a man of mixed fortunes. He was an antique dealer surrounded by treasures. People in this part of the world didn't part with anything if they could help it, so their houses were packed with heirlooms. Then the 'not parting with anything bit' came into action. It was like pulling teeth! Everyone was fascinated by his in-depth knowledge and ability to value 'Dad's old cupboard'. But when he asked if they wanted to part with it, the expressions became hard and the job became harder.

He knew exactly what they were thinking. *If it's worth that to him, what's it really worth?*

Nobody ever thought, *Oh you poor man, paying out to keep your shop open all those hours without selling anything.* They didn't understand 'shops'.

No, the attitude around here was, "Why have a huge room full of furniture and no-one living in it?"

The quirky yet irritating bell above the shop door clanged and Martin looked up.

His shop was filling up; it must be a coach tour. There hadn't been a group of tourists around here for ages. Not since the locals stood gawping back at them and frightened them off.

Martin rubbed his hands together in an unfortunate gesture which confirmed suspicions about his trade.

Margery approached the counter and smiled. The rest of the shop soon filled with people picking things up, gasping and putting them down with a thump. Margery had a distinguished man with her who was vaguely familiar. She said, "We are interested in a pair of stone lions from the old Hall in the next valley." She smiled again.

"Perhaps the bell as well," said Henry at her side.

Now, Martin had a problem. Those items had been too hard to sell and too heavy to move, so they were still in his back yard. To show these potential buyers he had to leave the rest of the customers in his shop unattended.

He quickly scanned the browsers, *they didn't seem a bad lot*, he thought, automatically using a sale-room term.

Taking a chance he ushered Margery and Henry into the back yard. Standing before the items, he said, "Be sorry to see these go. Really enjoyed owning them, very valuable they are."

"Is that why they are covered in dust and hidden behind bin bags?" asked Margery sweetly.

Martin recovered quickly, "Oh, that's an old trick of the trade to preserve the patination."

Margery and Henry stooped to examine the lions and Martin excused himself to return to the shop. *It was hardly likely that those two would run off with four tons of stone and bronze*, he thought. But the ones in the shop deserved *a good coat of looking at.*

Pushing aside a curtain, Martin returned to the shop. The suit of armour clanked towards him like some sort of barely controlled robot.

Geraldine was flinging metal-detector finds over her shoulder like a dog searching for a bone, and over in the far corner a scruffy little chap was winding a gramophone so fast that Mozart sounded like an electrocuted chipmunk!

Grabbing the suit of armour as it passed by, Martin managed to detach an arm. Racing in front of it he managed to lift the visor, only to find Cuthbert grinning at him.

"It's you!" the antique dealer said.

Martin had tried many times to buy from Cuthbert and others in the Valley, safe in the knowledge that they didn't know where his shop was. Now they knew!

A short bolt from a crossbow thudded into the counter near Martin. Ronald was disgusted, "This is a fake," he said, "A real one would have gone straight through."

Martin was at his wits end as Henry and Margery reappeared. It was part of the negotiation that the shop be cleared of all friends, acquaintances and mad relatives.

The strength of the Valley's negotiation was that 'They could always be invited back in' once the deal was struck and a discount was negotiated, because one of the lions appeared to have had its head stuck back on at a rakish angle.

Percy was left in charge of lifting the lions and the bell over a wall and taking them back to the Valley in his multi-purpose vehicle. Martin scratched his head as he surveyed the damage left by Percy, he had at last sold some heavy and awkward items, but by the time he had assessed wear and tear and paid for a new wall, he was out of pocket!

The lions were tied to each side of Percy's tractor, facing forward. The huge bronze bell was hung from the elevating arm sticking out behind him. Percy had also bought an old brass Fireman's helmet and it sat snugly on his head padded by his cap.

Chugging home happily, Percy found that if he made the tractor rock the bell would ring behind him. Off he went down the lanes, tracks clanking and bell ringing.

He almost didn't see Constable Beeching and his road block. The trouble was that the constable was so fat that you never knew whether he had set up a road-block or was just standing there! Percy managed to stop with a last *clang* of the bell behind him.

Constable Beeching waddled towards him licking his pencil. "What do you call this contraption then?" asked the constable in a feeble imitation of wit.

"Jezebel," answered Percy promptly. Pointing in turn to the lions, he added, "That's Je, that's ze," and then twisting around, he said, "That's bell."

The constable wrote everything down carefully, the pink tip of his tongue reflecting the level of concentration needed. The constable followed the interrogation manual faithfully, and asked, "What's your game then?"

Percy perked up even more, "Chess, I've just learnt it from Henry. Do you play?"

"Will this Henry vouch for you then?" asked Beeching.

Percy laughed, "Not since I took his queen."

The constable stopped writing. This was major! He racked his brains for the right charge. *If you fall asleep, it's napping, if you steal a goat and fall asleep, that's kidnapping. There must be a special word for Queen-napping*, he thought.

Then he looked at Percy. His car would never tow that thing and every time he put this character in a cell, he escaped!

This called for trickery. He remembered what his old sergeant had drilled into him, "The long arm of the law will always outreach the span of the bridge," or was it, the short span of the criminal mind? Or even...

"Ahem!" said Percy, "Will this take long. I am on my way to a fire you know."

The constable looked closely. *Oh, good grief*, he thought, *Special vehicle, shiny helmet and a bell. I'm impeding an emergency vehicle in the pursuit of its duty*.

Constable Beeching threw a hasty salute, and jumped into his car shouting, "Follow me," and set off down the lane with his siren blaring.

Percy muttered, "Okey-dokey." He followed for a few yards and promptly turned into a Farmer's gate and crossed the field.

Parking outside Cuthbert's he went inside, lifted the kettle and looked down into the cooking range. *That's the fire I'm on my way to*, he thought. *Never lie to the police!*

The hippo plodded along happily. Through experimental humming he had quite a repertoire now. *Pity there was no audience*, he thought. Life in the tunnels suited him fine. It was always dark and the walls had plenty of green stuff growing on them. Since he only ate at night anyway, this was a twenty-four hour buffet!

Margery had gathered everyone outside the Mandrake Arms for the occasion. Percy was on his way with the lions and Avril had her notebook ready. The morning sun was crisp and clear and everything was ready.

Geraldine was on hand with a magnifying glass and the scene was set. "I hope that twerp hurries up," said Geraldine, "I'm catching a flight this afternoon."

"Anywhere interesting?" asked Margery, watching the horizon.

Geraldine was pleased with herself. She had worked this into the conversation very nicely. "Oh, just a conference at one of the biggest museums in Europe. I am giving a lecture," she said proudly.

85

Margery answered absently, "Very nice, dear. Just don't lecture them the way you lecture us, and they might invite you again. Ah, here's Percy now."

Percy's appearance was heralded by a cloud of black smoke, the clattering of tracks and the tolling of the huge bell.

"One of the tractors of the apocalypse," muttered Geraldine, sulking.

One by one the lions were lifted into place each side of the door of the Mandrake Arms. Geraldine examined them minutely from all angles before they were finally lowered.

She shook her head quite pleased to return a crushing remark to Margery. "Nope!" she said, "Nothing at all. No inscription, no clues, nothing!"

Margery was somewhat deflated. Still, they looked wonderful in their new home.

"Where do you want the bell?" asked Percy.

Henry coughed and stepped forward. The bell had actually saved his life when Mandrake Hall collapsed around him. "I rather thought that we could mount it on a wooden frame as an exhibit. It would look wonderful near the horse trough," he announced.

Everyone agreed and Percy moved it over to its new site. No-one was looking when Percy gave the old bronze bell a rub with his sleeve, but they all turned, when he said, "Ooh look. There's writing on it!"

Geraldine left for her lecture tour and the women took turns cleaning the huge bell with a variety of chemical and abrasive cleaners. Mrs Biggle seemed hurt that her stock didn't include any *ancient bell restorative cleaner* but she sold them some scouring powder and cotton buds anyway.

Gradually the embossed letters were revealed. Henry walked slowly around the girth of the bell and read out aloud as he walked. "My sound is silver when I'm tolled, though made of brass my heart is gold."

The silence was broken by a shriek. Margery grabbed a shovel and yelled, "It's under the old church!" and off she went.

Henry scratched his head and said, "It wasn't from the church. It was from the Hall."

Mrs. Biggle said, "It was taken from the old church to use as an alarm on top of the Hall. The old owner thought that the Russians were coming."

Henry looked at her, "Is that true?"

Mrs. Biggle replied, "Hope so! I've still got some foul-smelling cigarettes in stock, ready for them."

Cuthbert watched the lions being placed with mixed feelings. They had been part of his past and after all, he *was* partly responsible for the demise of the Hall. He didn't really hold with all this re-positioning of things around the Valley. Things should stay where they're put. That's how people got lost when a landmark wasn't on the right land, or even worse, when it was the right mark on the wrong land.

Chapter 24

Geraldine was feeling rather fraught. Life in the Valley didn't prepare anyone for the chaos of modern living. Where was everyone going? And what's the rush?

Jostled by crowds and almost pushed under trams, Geraldine stopped for coffee. Her languages were rusty, so she pointed at the illustrations of different blends near the poster with an animal on it. The coffee came with a free tubular biscuit with chocolate inside it. Geraldine was reminded of a section of sewer pipe and put it to one side.

Sipping the coffee and watching humanity surge past, her eyes were drawn back to the poster with the animal on it. It was a lion and above it was the word for 'wanted'. Who on earth would advertise for a lion? *Perhaps it was a wanted poster,* she thought, giggling at the thought of a lion with a handkerchief over its face robbing a bank. Perhaps its accomplice was a kangaroo and they were ordered to fill its pouch!

The man on the next table gave her a strange look as she laughed out loud. Leaving some money on the table, Geraldine left the café. Now that she had seen one poster, she began to see them everywhere. Not always a lion though. She spotted one for a llama and another for an elephant!

Seeing the British Embassy ahead, she entered and asked about the posters. Something was niggling away at her about them.

The local girl at reception pointed out several different ones on the reception room walls and happily translated them. Apparently, it was for the annual circus competition. A huge event, still really big in Europe, and the main contender had gone missing. The posters not only advertised the event, but asked people to look out for strange animals in case they had all become separated.

Geraldine felt slightly queasy as she asked, "Where does this take place?"

The girl answered brightly, "Oh it is at Cutt-berts-Hausen every year, a little village near to Vallee on the border."

Geraldine just gawped. Aunt Edith hadn't given up the circus. *She had sent it on ahead*!

Instead of Cutt-berts-Hausen, near Vallee, some idiot had redirected it to Cuthbert's house, the Valley!

Geraldine wandered off to find a phone.

When the call reached the Valley everyone was gathered in the Mandrake Arms trying to dissuade Margery from digging up the bodies under the old church.

Margery answered the phone and waved for silence. The bar hushed as Margery's eyes opened even wider than when she spoke of gold. "Thank you dear," she said, "Try to find out all you can please." She hung up.

Margery explained the things Geraldine had discovered, and finished with, "Apparently it's the biggest event of the circus year and Aunt Edith wins it every year. She is running around Europe looking to find her circus in time for the judging after some fool sent the lot to the wrong place."

The hubbub of conversation eased somewhat, when Percy said, "Huh, small world isn't it? One of my cousin's works at an airport over there somewhere."

The next phone call from Geraldine was a real mixed blessing.

As Margery put it, "We've got good news and bad news."

Percy jumped up and down shouting, "Oh! Oh I know. The good news is that we've won ten million pounds and the bad news is it's all in one-pound coins."

Margery paused and waited for her sanity to catch up, but Mrs. Biggle joined in, "No Percy, the good news is that the Valley Mafia have all been expelled. The bad news is that I can't reach to clean the camera lens."

Ronald tried, "The good news is that the pub is having topless bar-staff. The bad news is that Cuthbert has just got a job here."

Margery could see Cuthbert waiting to retaliate and Percy was starting to jump up and down again, so she went down into the cellar to change a barrel over. She loved the cool atmosphere of the cellar. It was even cooler now that the men had taken the wall down. How come they could burst with energy when a job began, but all have *better things to do* when it needed finishing? Margery pottered happily with the metal cask and started humming *Bolero* to herself. The open tunnel gave it an echo and she could almost believe that a bass section had joined in.

Back in the bar when Margery returned everyone seemed to be

leaning back in their chairs and wiping their eyes. With any luck, the moment had passed and she could speak. "The good news is," she began with a *don't you dare* glare at Percy, "The judges are prepared to come over here and judge the circus in the Valley."

The room filled with an appreciative murmur. "The bad news is," she continued, "The circus staff are scattered about all over Europe looking for the animals and they cannot be reached."

Ronald said, "Well, that's it then. She won't win this year."

Margery put her hand up, "Not unless we win it for her."

Complete absence of sound only usually occurs in the deepest mines, or in outer space. The bar at the Mandrake Arms had just joined these god-forsaken places and yet it was full of people!

"Typical daft woman's idea," barked the Captain. He had waited several hours to voice his opinion and was safely tucked away in Cuthbert's kitchen when he risked it.

Cuthbert wasn't so daring. He never knew where Margery might pop up from next.

"Might be fun," hazarded Henry, ignoring the slight against his wife.

Cuthbert looked at him in astonishment. "Are you seriously thinking about it?"

Henry looked around the table. "Look," he began, "Since I came to this valley I have had more adventures than I ever had as a front-line journalist. They seem to work out all right, don't they?"

Heads nodded and smiles appeared. "That's it boys," said Margery as she walked from another room, "You know it makes sense." Patting her husband on the shoulder and throwing the Captain a withering look, she smiled at Cuthbert and left via the front door.

"Can I work with the penguins?" asked Percy.

"We haven't got any penguins," said Cuthbert.

"Yes we have," insisted Percy.

"I'm rather good with camels, actually," stated the Captain.

Cuthbert took a breath, "We haven't any of those either."

"Yes we have," insisted the Captain and Percy.

"I don't fancy that tiger much," said Ronald.

"We haven't got one of those either" snapped Cuthbert.

"Yes we have," insisted everybody.

90

Henry looked at Cuthbert, and asked, "Don't you *ever* look inside your outbuildings?"

Cuthbert shifted uncomfortably, "Not if I can help it. Last time I looked I found a body I had forgotten to bury."

Henry was shocked, "How did you miss it?"

"It was behind another one I forgot about," said Cuthbert mournfully.

Ronald commented, "Well, that's the tiger fed anyway!"

Margery was briefing her potential handlers. "Make sure you register all allergies, girls," she was saying. "We can leave the men with anything angry, noisy or violent. We will concentrate on the 'fluffy bunny' side of things."

Arkle shifted on her chair. "Er, fluffy bunnies don't seem to last long after I stroke them," she said shame-faced.

"Oh," said Margery, "Double-act with the gorilla dear?"

Arkle brightened.

Mrs. Biggle confided that she had been inviting the doves in off her roof and doing tricks with them, and she could refine that. "I've even got the black one wiping his feet before he comes in," she announced proudly.

Margery was quite taken with the Shetland pony, so that was her settled. Avril had found that she could confide in the llama and they had many a happy chat over the fence. Geraldine would take a while to get back, so she didn't really have time to get involved, and Elspeth was already scouring her kettles and hot-dog grills.

The daily feeding round was an exciting time now. Everyone discussed their plans as they worked, and each one tried to predict what the animals could do.

The elephant could walk around the ring flapping its ears and waving its trunk. The giraffe could walk around the ring being a giraffe and the hippo could… Where *was* the hippo?

Gradually they began to realise that walking the animals in circles would not win the circus competition. They needed gimmicks, they needed routines. The women perked up, *they* needed costumes!

Chapter 25

The road gang had planned an assault on the treasure site. A large rubbish collecting truck trundled its way into the village. Hidden in the back were, One lung Louie and Swivelling Simon.'

Marvin rode in the front as a passenger and Buster was driving. Red Ronnie was also there. He was in their thoughts, because revolution was in the air. The rubbish truck pulled up outside the Mandrake Arms just as the men had returned for refreshments for the women.

Henry watched the truck approach, and said, "That's strange!"

"What's that?" asked the Captain.

Henry nodded at the vehicle, "Never seen one of those in the Valley before. Anything spare out here either gets eaten or re-used."

Percy seemed to agree. Wandering over to the passenger side of the cab he leant against a box of large buttons, all in prominent colours. "Morning Marvin. Taking the new car out for a spin?" he asked.

Marvin was 'on duty' and he had an employee beside him. "It's Mr. Middlewick to you. And this is a state of the art refuse truck. Please stand away from it."

Percy's eyes widened, "State of the art, eh! I can't imagine that thing hung on someone's wall somehow."

Buster leaned over inside the cab, and said, "It even talks!"

Percy's eyebrows disappeared under his cap. "A talking truck, eh! Didn't Noddy have one of those?"

Buster didn't remember Noddy, but then he had always been confused by the Teletubbies! "I'll show you," he said, and put the truck in reverse.

Percy jumped as a metallic voice announced, *This vehicle is reversing. This vehicle is reversing.* He was impressed. "Wow!" he said as the truck moved forward again, "What does this one do?"

Marvin shouted, "Don't touch that," as Percy pressed the red button. A low rumbling came from the bowels of the truck.

Marvin looked at Buster and yelled, "What's he done?"

Buster shrugged, "I don't know, it's my first day," and began leafing through the manual.

In the back, Simon's eye began to swivel. "All those years in pipes and tunnels never bothered me, but this is different somehow. I could swear that the walls are closing in."

Buster read through the manual methodically until he reached an interesting bit. "The -mechanical- compactor- is- capable- of- crushing-the- whole- rear- section- and- its- contents- into- a- space -of- just- a-few- inches." He gazed at the illustration in awe and then glanced at Marvin.

Marvin had gone really pale and his jaw hung as if the elastic had snapped. A frantic hammering from inside stung everyone into action.

Percy pressed the red button again and the rumbling stopped. The green button started the rumbling off again, but it seemed to be going the other way. That left the blue button! Percy savoured the moment and then pressed it.

"What's he done, what's he done now?" yelled Marvin.

Buster ponderously started to read again, "The -revolution -will-begin-when-all-the-brothers-are-… Sorry, wrong leaflet."

Meanwhile, Percy watched in utter fascination as one end of the refuse truck started to lift, becoming a giant 'tipper truck'.

Mrs. Biggle walked past just as the back of the machine was vertical and Louie and Simon tumbled out onto the road. "Oh! Goody," she said, "A vending machine for men; about time," and she began to rummage in her purse for some loose change.

Buster looked up as a distant memory stirred in his subconscious. Percy was strolling away grinning and he was accompanied by a s*lap, slap* sound as he walked.

Marvin indicated weakly that they should *All climb back on board, lower the back, return to the cabin and give up for today.*

Not bad for one floppy hand movement!

Chapter 26

The afternoon was spent having a picnic and discussing what exactly the animals were capable of. After a few attempts, Henry banned the expression, *being cute*.

The women seemed fixated on some sort of 'Cruft's' event where everyone wore national dress and walked in circles with a thing on a string. The men, being the competitive side of the gender war, realised that far more would be needed to win such a prestigious event.

Ronald suggested a Buffalo Bill type circus where the Indians attacked and the cowboys rode in to the rescue. The ladies could wear gingham dresses and say *Aww shucks mister* before swooning in gratitude. Arkle stood up and everyone moved away from Ronald. Fortunately she went to move the elephant; it was blocking the sun, and she then sat down quietly.

Most people would have prodded the thing until it got up, but Arkle simply lifted one end and turned it through its axis.

Avril spoke next, she pointed out that by the time the Indians had been massacred and become an endangered race and inter-racial wars over settlers rights had been fought, all the humans would be dead and the animals wouldn't have put in an appearance.

"I would have ridden a horse," said Ronald moodily.

Henry proposed a Coliseum theme, where all the animals performed in an arena setting and the men dressed as gladiators.

Margery complained that the women seemed to be *back to swooning again*.

Cuthbert wasn't really taking part in the discussion. For one thing he didn't see where he would fit in, as all the animals ignored him. Another distraction was the fact that he had found another body. Somewhere, on the edge of his thoughts, something niggled at him. He began to pay attention and he heard it again.

Interrupting the Captain's inspirational flow, Cuthbert asked, "What big-top?"

The Captain spluttered, annoyed at being interrupted. "Our big-top, the one we will perform under, tradition, you know," he assured the others.

Cuthbert said, "We haven't got one, or is that in an out-building

94

somewhere as well?"

Glances were exchanged. Heads were shaken, *Poor Cuthbert, never quite there with the rest of us*, seemed to be the prevailing thought. Then Henry asked 'the big one'. "We haven't got one, have we?" Cuthbert was reinstated as the bottom rung in the thinking hierarchy.

The women were confident that the problem could be solved. Cuthbert had agreed that the cinema's largest building could be used and the women could drape the inside with hanging swags of material. If the material was decorated with fetching stripes it would look like a big-top from inside!

Margery gathered her troops for a foraging raid. All curtains, bedding, and large pyjamas were expected to be donated. Elspeth promised to 'fire-up' the old horse drawn field kitchen to use for boiling and dyeing. The men mentally crossed off the soup at the next Winter Gala. Cuthbert and Percy walked back to the farm. Somehow the women were there ahead of them, and they were armed!

Each lady was carrying a wicker basket like a shield in one hand, and a large wooden spoon in the other. Cuthbert politely and suspiciously let them in. The women declined the offer of tea and got right to business.

"We thought we would start with you two," said Margery.

"Oh, thank you," said Percy sarcastically. Was it his imagination or was there a woman each side of him?

Cuthbert played a few tunes in his head waiting for someone to explain things.

Margery lost patience and said, "Curtains, Cuthbert!"

Percy laughed out loud, "That's an ancestor you kept quiet about mate."

The women closed in on him. Margery tried again, "Cuthbert, focus," she said, and, "We discussed this. We need everyone's curtains and bedding to make the striped awnings. We're starting with you."

Cuthbert's face cleared, "Oh yes, I remember. What can I do for you?"

Margery stared at him in amazement. The women shook their heads like a synchronised nodding dog team.

"Curtains Cuthbert, and bedding," shrieked Margery.

Cuthbert's reply was calm, but in terms of feminist gunpowder it was an incandescent spark. "Yes," he said, "But what can *we* do for you?"

Margery tightened her grip on her wash basket, causing it to twist out of shape. Her spoon was rising slowly and her eyes had settled into a homicidal glaze.

"Just a minute, Margery," Elspeth stepped in front of Cuthbert. She stared him straight in the eye and said, "Curtains," not a flicker. She tried, "Bedding" - no reaction, either. Her last resort was, "Little lacy covers to put under flower vases," absolutely blank.

Elspeth staggered backwards. To a housewife of her sensibilities she had entered Sodom and Gomorrah! She spluttered, "These *bachelors* don't have any of the necessities."

The women would have crossed themselves, but they already had their hands full. Cuthbert and Percy watched in silence as the women edged away and out of the door, never taking their eyes off the two men. The door slammed behind them.

"Huh! Women," spat Percy.

"What do they know?" Cuthbert relaxed and grinned at his friend. "I thought that went rather well."

Percy put the kettle on. "Definitely, what on earth would we wipe our boots on if we didn't have curtains?"

Chapter 27

Back in the cabin, the atmosphere was tense. The drains Inspector had not been part of the now infamous 'refuse truck raid'. He had pieced together the incident and was trying to keep the two sides apart.

"You could have killed us," accused Louie.

"I was driving," pleaded Buster. "What sort of idiot puts the buttons on the outside anyway?"

The drains Inspector sucked air through his teeth at this, "Careful lad, walls have ears," he whispered. "The authority knows best," he added loudly for good measure.

Buster had just about had it and he stood up, disturbing the smog. "It's a good job the walls have got ears, because this team is short of eyes, brains and lungs!"

The team were horrified. This was personal!

"Be very careful, my lad," hissed Swivelling Simon. "In the land of the blind, the one-eyed man is King."

"Yes, yes," said One-lung Louie, desperate for something to match it. "Hurr, when the air runs out, the lone lung lad lasts longest, hurr."

The drains Inspector asked suspiciously, "What do you mean *brains*?"

Buster looked shocked, "Oh I didn't mean you, drains Inspector!"

*

Geraldine rang again that night. With some help from the Ambassador and the museum authorities, she had persuaded the judges to come to the Valley and judge the circus where it was. They could stay at the Mandrake Arms, but someone would have to meet them at the airport.

They were VIP's so they would need a chauffeur.

Margery had no idea where to find a chauffeur, but as Geraldine pointed out, "If you borrow Marvin's car, all you need is someone who owns a hat!"

Henry was chosen to talk to Marvin about the loan of the car, but the only person he could find to accompany him was Percy.

Marvin listened patiently as Henry pushed all the right buttons. Good for the Valley's image, publicity for the local authority, etc, etc.

97

Marvin liked what he was hearing, but he wished the little scruffy one would stop wandering about. Marvin thought he would try some leverage. He asked Henry directly, "What do you know about this gold buried under the high street? Man to man." He added with a glance at Percy, "Or in his case, man to mascot."

Percy began to study the wall. "Another list eh, Marvin. What is it this time, assassination of tea-ladies or addresses to send poisoned paper-clips?"

Marvin's expression froze. He had forgotten that this idiot was privy to his past.

Percy grinned at him. "I'll just put my name here under Doreeen, shall I?"

Marvin handed over the keys to Henry, as a 'show of good faith, you understand'.

Henry accepted them gratefully, and leaned forward across the desk. "Between you, me, and the gatepost," he said. "If it exists, it could be anywhere. Cuthbert certainly doesn't know. There was a vague telegram mentioning a legacy and the circus dropped on his doorstep."

Henry sat back, asking, "How did *you* get on to it?"

Marvin squirmed. "It was an anonymous phone call," he admitted. "Someone offered me half, if I could find it using the authority as cover."

Henry slipped into journalist mode, adopted a human expression and began to collect ammunition for later. "How did he phrase it?"

Marvin was taken aback and had to think hard to remember, "It was old-fashioned," he said slowly, "Something about the proceeds of the Bolsheviks being shared between the proletariat before the circle, or something."

"Revolution?" suggested Henry.

Marvin gaped, "How did you know?"

Henry looked at Percy, "What do you make of it?"

Percy took a pamphlet from his pocket and waved it, "Sounds like a quote from Red Ronnie to me."

Chapter 28

When Henry returned to the Mandrake Arms, Margery nearly fainted.

"You should be at the airport," she said through gritted teeth. "The judges need collecting."

Henry waved a hand, "All taken care of. There was only one of us who owned a hat."

Margery sat down heavily, "Oh my godfathers. Please tell me that you didn't send Percy." Henry opened his mouth, but instinct closed it again and he sat down quietly. "How could you?" wailed Margery. "They will be judging the circus!"

Ronald said, "Perhaps they will assume that we've sent one of the clowns." Then *he* shut up too.

Modern cars are strange, thought Percy. How do you feel at one with the road when you can't hear the engine? It didn't even vibrate properly. He pulled a few handles when he first got in, because his new brass helmet caught on the roof. His seat slid forward, then it slid back. When his arms could reach the steering wheel his legs couldn't reach the pedals, and when his feet could reach the pedals he was close enough to steer with his teeth!

After compromising by reclining at a forty-five degree angle, he set off. Music came from speakers all around the car, which was fine until someone announced the next programme. Suddenly Percy had a car full of people, there were voices everywhere!

The airport was busy when Percy arrived, but he managed to park right outside by terrifying a couple with an expensive pile of luggage by demonstrating his parking skills.

Sitting there, Percy watched as people held up pieces of cardboard and someone coming out of the doors would rush up and embrace them. He assumed that it was some sort of dating agency and you picked whichever one you fancied. *Must try that one day,* he thought. After all the people had picked new partners for the weekend, there were only three people left.

Percy wasn't surprised, they looked like an undertakers convention; perhaps Cuthbert knew them? It must have been embarrassing not to be picked, and now they were coming this way!

The tall woman led the way and the two sombre men followed.

Percy was fascinated, one of the men looked like a cross between a bloodhound and a melted candle. The other one wasn't very different really.

The woman asked, "Are you waiting for us?"

Percy suspected that he was, but he wasn't getting the blame for anything, "I don't know; who are you?"

The woman said, "We are the circus judges."

Percy beamed, "In that case, yes I am, hop in."

The woman looked at him expectantly, "Shouldn't you open the door?"

Percy looked back at her, "I did, that's how *I* got in."

The two men climbed into the back; the tall woman went round to sit with Percy in the front. Just as Percy *revved up* the woman pointed past him, and said, "Luggage."

Percy assumed that she was checking her pronunciation and agreed. "That's right, *luggage*. Bags, cases, holdalls. It mostly means the same thing," and he drove off!

They were well behaved passengers, Percy had to grant them that, although what Marvin would make of the fake fingernails embedded in his dashboard, he couldn't imagine.

Pulling up outside the Mandrake Arms, Percy forgot about the large stone lions he had recently placed outside. With a *whoops* and a swerve, he avoided them nicely, but he and the woman seemed to have developed a bubble-gum habit.

The white balloons slowly deflated and the woman looked archly at Percy, "Air-*luggage*, I presume!"

Chapter 29

Inside with Margery and the women fussing around them, things became more normal. Henry was sent to the airport to collect the bags and Percy was definitely not offered a drink.

The woman introduced them. Indicating each man in turn, she said. "This is Herr Heer and this is Herr There. I am neither heer nor there, I am Olga."

The Valley ladies loved her. She explained that she was also the interpreter and that the two men would not speak, to maintain their impartiality. Margery showed them to their rooms.

Downstairs in the bar, Cuthbert asked Percy, "Not impressed with modern motoring then?"

"Not really," he admitted. "That car had everything, it even had a television on the dashboard, but it seemed to be a programme about making maps."

"Look Cuthbert," Henry's voice was reasonable, but pleading, "The animals don't hate you, they need a firm hand, show them who is the master; take the bull by the horns."

Cuthbert looked at Percy, "Have we got a bull?"

Percy said, "There's a hippo around somewhere."

Henry gently led Cuthbert over to the giraffe. "There is no record of a giraffe ever harming a human be… anyone, ever," he said.

The Captain looked doubtful and offered, "Except for that incident when Squiffy and his chums were trampled in the great stampede."

Henry shot him a warning look and the Captain qualified it with, "Of course, they were mostly rhinos and Squiffy shouldn't have shot one of them, but there was a giraffe in there somewhere. It was probably the look-out."

Cuthbert looked up at the expanse of neck reaching for more of his thatch. He felt like Jack at the bottom of the beanstalk. With a faint swishing sound, the giraffe brought its head down in an arc. It nuzzled Henry fondly and batted its eye-lashes at him.

Henry saw his reflection in the chocolate brown eyes and felt at peace. Cuthbert however, found that the giraffe had planted its two back feet on his two only feet and he was trapped at eye level with its short tail, and *the tail was lifting*!

Henry rushed Cuthbert away.

The lion growled as they passed him and flicked out his claws like an assassin in the dark. A heavy rumbling deterred them from the gorilla's room, and the elephant had already filled its trunk with water. Henry sat on the stile. Cuthbert stood by him like a schoolboy, having to explain exactly where the rest of the class had gone during the map reading exercise.

Henry studied Cuthbert and asked, "Have you an affinity with any creature?"

Cuthbert thought for a moment. "I have an argument with a crow," he offered.

Henry tried, "Rats, mice?"

Cuthbert sighed, "They don't even notice me. They think *I'm* the lodger."

Henry scanned the farmyard, it was hopeless. He had tried Cuthbert with the monkeys, but they swung on his ears. The Shetland pony had walked between his legs and the snake had displayed a hissy-fit.

Cuthbert had a suggestion, "Perhaps they can smell death on me?"

Henry stared, "Cuthbert, no-one can smell death on you. You keep forgetting to bury them!"

The doves and the crow clattered overhead, but detoured around Cuthbert's air-space. The hippo had just finished a rendition of a cello concerto which had even caused the stones to vibrate in sympathy. He entertained his fantasy for a moment.

What if he became famous? His family were mostly known for lumbering across plains and winning the Hog-wallowing contest on the Masai Mara. He could be the first with his name in lights! Then it struck him. *What was his name?* How would his family know he was famous?

The problems mounted. He didn't have a name. His parents didn't have names. There was no point putting his unknown name up in lights, because his family had no electricity. His face on a poster wouldn't help. All his family bore an uncanny resemblance to each other. No-one ever held an identity parade in their neck of the desert. Lowering his head, the hippo moved on slowly with only the funeral march for company.

Henry was taking a chance. He knew Percy wanted to work with the penguins, but they were the only harmless thing left for Cuthbert to handle. The birds had formed a colony at the other side of the duck pond.

Watching one of the penguins waddle away from them, Cuthbert asked, "Where's Ronald?"

Henry replied, "Funny, I was just wondering the same thing!"

They took it in turns to throw a fish into the duck-pond. Henry's throw was received by flapping, shrieking, and beautifully executed dives to retrieve it. Cuthbert's fish flickered briefly in the air and landed with a splat. How embarrassing, to spend your life as a fish and then be rejected as a meal. If it hadn't been dead it may have swum back for another go!

Cuthbert was annoyed, picking up another fish he carried it personally around the pond to hand-deliver it. The penguins saw him coming and formed *line of battle*, then as he neared they executed a synchronised right turn and waddled into the tunnels in single file.

"Oh, marvellous," sighed Henry. "And here comes Percy."

The hippo had just about come to terms with life as a hippo. The obvious conclusion was that if you were famous but unknown, then you would be equally unknown if you were not famous. So basically, a hippo always played on a level playing field because they weren't good at going uphill!

He was just realising that he would never hold a pen to write these great thoughts down and that would explain why there were no great hippo philosophers, when the first of the penguins appeared in front of him.

Percy slapped across to the pond and smiled at Henry and Cuthbert. Then he focused on the far side of the pond, just as the last *dinner jacket tail* disappeared into a tunnel. Placing his bucket of fish on the ground Percy waited for Cuthbert to return with his rejected offering still in his hand.

Cuthbert shrugged an apology when he reached Percy, but was interrupted by Percy hitting him over the head with a cod before storming off. Cuthbert wiped off a smear of silvery fragments and Henry commented, "Scales of justice eh?"

The hippo had lots of time for these little fellers. They had the same identity crisis as the hippos. What was the point of shouting "Stop that bird!" in the middle of a penguin colony?

The group ambled along the tunnel together with the hippo, timing the pendulous swing of his head with the movement of the penguins rocking from side to side. The hippo hummed as they walked, and he noticed that the penguins were keeping time with the music! Then one little feller broke away, stuck out his wings and tried a pirouette! The rest formed up into two ranks facing each other and bowed!

Instinctively the hippo changed the tempo. Tchaikovsky had an immediate effect, the penguins eyes glazed over and the movements became fluid. They wove in and out of formation and never missed a beat.

This is phenomenal, thought the hippo. *This is one for the autobiography.* Then he felt depressed as he remembered all the other reasons against him, plus one more which had only just occurred to him. *Most agents have their offices on the first floor!*

Chapter 30

The bar in the Mandrake Arms was full. Everyone was there to officially welcome the judges and make a good impression. Olga, the translator, constantly leaned over to explain something to the judges, and they nodded silently in return. Ronald and Olga had really hit it off and were seen huddled together in a corner.

Apparently, she had learned to speak English so that she could travel and eventually meet her father. Ronald listened in fascination as the romantic tale unfolded.

During the cold war Olga's mother had met a foreign adventurer on a secret mission and they had fallen in love. The mysterious spy had been called away and was never seen again, but it was her mission to find him and demand all the back alimony he owed! Ronald gulped as he remembered a tryst behind the tractor factory, and hid behind Cuthbert for the rest of the evening.

It wasn't long before Percy noticed that after a speech, and anyone calling out *hear hear*, one of the judges would rise, click his heels together and empty his glass.

Percy nudged Henry and they both watched before Henry solved the matter. "That one must be Herr Heer," he said. "Every time someone shouts, 'hear hear' he thinks they are toasting him, so he returns the compliment." Percy liked that and soon became very enthusiastic in praising other people's speeches.

The judge was bobbing up and down like a meerkat and downing little glasses of clear liquid. Soon, the atmosphere became more relaxed and the judge started to follow the tradition of his homeland and began throwing the empty glass into the fireplace. Unfortunately, this room had been modernised and the radiator took quite a bit of damage.

After the speeches Olga stood up wearing a very loud patterned dress, which Margery referred to as *Zebra road kill*, and thanked their hosts for making them welcome. She then praised the whole Valley for its dedication to the circus and acknowledged past circus acts which originated here.

The locals looked at each other, wondering how much had been lost in translation. She then paused for dramatic effect and announced,

"The grandson of the Great Plumm." She was clapping furiously and so were the judges.

The locals just gawped as Percy went to the front and took a bow. Cuthbert turned to Henry and asked, "They've heard of him out there?"

Henry noticed one of the judges wipe a tear from his eye, and replied, "Oh they've heard of him all right."

Percy pulled out a seat, sat down and shuffled. The judges applauded again, they seemed to recognise something! Percy began, "Normally, I wouldn't brag about my family," The crowd hissed. "But the circus connection cannot be ignored. My grandfather was The Great Albert Plumm, an escapologist years ahead of his time. He had been obsessed with escaping, after spending his first day at school. Soon he was amazing the world with his miracle escapes and apparently impossible feats. He had escaped from the Tower of London and the Bastille. Alcatraz couldn't hold him and neither could Devils Island. The crowned heads of Europe watched his escapes. In fact some of them came to wish they had paid more attention to their jewellery at the time! He became really famous when he was asked to appear at a sinister castle in a place called Transylvania."

The interpreter and the judges all shivered at the mention of the place, but due to the delay in translation, it was more of a Mexican tremble.

Percy continued. "What he didn't know was that a beautiful princess was being held captive in the castle and he was the only one who could get close to her. He arrived after dark during a thunderstorm and met the owner of the castle, Count Yerb Lessings. The Count had a penchant for long cloaks and dramatic entrances. At dinner that night, the three of them dined at a very long table with the Count at one end, Albert at the other and the princess in the middle. A log fire blazed and the food was brought by silent servants. Conversation was difficult, because of the length of the table, and was also hindered by the fact that all three of them spoke a different language. Later that night, the door to my grandfather's room crashed open. But he was gone! The Count scoured the castle, the princess was also missing. The clatter of hooves brought everyone out into the courtyard, a carriage stolen from the Count was leaving by the front gate, and the servants began shooting fire arrows after it. The horses shied sideways and broke the traces. The carriage carried on straight ahead and went over the cliff like a blazing comet, to crash hundreds of feet below." The interpreter and the judges indulged in a little Mexican weep now. "In the morning the wreckage was still smoking, but of the bodies, there was no sign. The princess turned up at her family home in perfect health, but my Grandfather was never seen again."

Percy bowed his head and sucked the maximum amount of pathos out of the moment, before leaving the stage to the applause of the judges and the narrowed eyes of the locals.

As if by telepathy Cuthbert, Henry, the Captain, and Ronald formed a cordon around Percy and escorted him to a quiet corner.

"Alright Percy," snarled Ronald, "We've not heard that one before."

"Why are we suspicious?"

Percy actually looked sheepish! "Well," he admitted, "It was all a bit of a misunderstanding. Albert decided to take advantage of a gap-year before being unemployed full-time, and he went backpacking across Europe. Somewhere deep inside a forest this coach pulled up and offered him a lift. The chap inside was the escape artist and he asked my Grandfather to deliver a note of apology to the Count. Basically it said, *Can't make it mate, and had a better offer from Count Yer-Cash. Disappear for you later* The coach dropped Albert off at the gates and everyone assumed he was the escapologist. Not one of them spoke the same language and no-one else could read the note, so they assumed that it was dietary requirements and sent it to the cook. Anyway, it turned out that the princess wasn't particularly beautiful at all and she had a voice like a diamond on glass. She assumed that the visitor had come to rescue her and the Count was praying that he had! So that night, all the doors were left unlocked and the carriage and horses were left ready. Just as my Granddad went in search of the privy, the princess made her move. Kicking in doors until she found the stairs, she jumped onto the back of one of the horses and raced away with the carriage bouncing along behind. The servants fired fire arrows to make sure that the horses kept going and Albert walked out to see what all the fuss was about! The princess clung on to the horse when the traces snapped, and the empty blazing carriage went over the cliff. The servants quickly closed the doors and Albert was outside, so he carried on with his holiday and walked away. The princess arrived home and a legend was born."

Chapter 31

The next morning Cuthbert came down to find Percy cooking breakfast, and he seemed to be singing.

On closer inspection, it was actually chanting, quite catchy too, and Cuthbert found himself joining in with "Cage Rage! Cage rage!" Cuthbert heaved the kettle onto the cooking range and addressed Percy, "Where did you learn that?"

Percy waved a vague hand, "From that lot out there."

Cuthbert tried to look into the farmyard but the window was steamed up, so he opened the door.

The group of people outside were walking in a circle, holding placards above their heads, chanting, "Cage-rage! Cage rage!"

They instantly spotted Cuthbert and broke the circle to cluster around him, led by a bearded man with mud oozing through his toes due to sandals not being recommended farmyard footwear.

"What do you say to this?" he demanded, pumping his placard up and down. Cuthbert's neutral expression registered that the sign was facing away from him, so a response really didn't seem in order, so he just stared. "Ha, cat got your tongue eh?" ranted the man.

The woman beside him was appalled. "Roger; how could you?" she asked. "We never denigrate any animal species; you make fluffy kittens sound like the aggressors, shame on you."

The bearded man spluttered, "I'm not the one at fault woman, he's the one with animals in cages."

"He only has one cage," came a voice from the back.

"He referred to you as *woman*," called another voice, "That's misogynist, that is."

A chorus of voices began, "My sign doesn't mention that."

"Mine neither."

"Mine says we need a bill of rights. Does that only apply to ducks?"

The bearded man was whipping himself into a state as the man in the doorway repelled all attempts to blacken his name and somehow bounced it all back onto him. "Shut up all of you, this is becoming a circus."

"We know it's a circus, that's why we're here."

"Who put him in charge?"

Roger, the man with the beard and the slimy feet, growled as he swung his placard. The assembly gasped at this overt display of violence. Cuthbert stepped back slightly and the man completed a three hundred and sixty degree turn, only to make contact with the kitten lady, who promptly clubbed him with the handle of her *Puppies and Peace* poster.

Cuthbert watched for a few more minutes, as the melee developed into a free for all, and the factions battled their way down his farm track.

Re-entering the kitchen with the door closed behind him, he sat in front of the breakfast Percy had placed before him.

Percy raised an eyebrow, "Did you have a word with them?"

"No need," said Cuthbert. "They seemed to have plenty of their own."

Chapter 32

Margery was secretive all evening, and had been rather tense. The women had been leaving the bar on a regular basis and now all was revealed. In fact, more than was intended at one point! Margery strode into the centre of the room in her costume. There were legs, and feathers; lots of feathers and more legs. Then there were the legs!

The men had never seen such legs, Margery had always been a beauty, but this simply said, *Hah! Look what you lot missed!* As his wife paraded, Henry watched the others in amusement. "Nice effect, eh! Chaps?"

Ronald blurted, "Nice feathers."

The Captain said dreamily, "Finest feathers I've ever seen."

"Lovely feathers," risked Percy.

Cuthbert managed, "Longest feathers I've ever seen."

The rest of the costumes were a bit of an anticlimax, but the women had worked so hard that riotous applause greeted every offering. Spangles sparkled, sequins shimmered, and bits fell off at surprising moments.

Nobody noticed a huge hand appear around Cuthbert's mouth and him being lifted off his feet, before disappearing. Percy turned to nudge Cuthbert, but his elbow swung through thin air, which surprisingly smelled of horse!

Automatically checking the floor in case his friend had passed out, he shrugged and continued to watch the show.

Margery swept into the room again like some sexy cartoon ostrich, and announced, "Okay Cuthbert, we've shown you ours, now show me yours!"

The room froze! Drinks didn't reach lips and thoughts stayed well away from brains. Cuthbert shambled into the room, his face as red as his coat. His funeral top-hat shone and his old farm boots sparkled beneath his white trousers; he gripped his whip tightly.

The audience stared at Cuthbert, ringmaster personified!

As the room exploded into applause, Henry leaned across to the men and explained, "Since none of the animals can stand him, we thought that if we stood him in the middle they would all keep to the outside of the ring, where we can see them."

110

Cuthbert gained in confidence at the attention he was getting and swung his whip dramatically, clearing one of Margery's shelves of clean glasses and causing her to lose a few feathers!

Chapter 33

The road gang had declared a truce. It was generally agreed that Red Ronnie had been causing trouble amongst them, and that *Politics had no part in drains*. The things politicians said was another matter, but that would be the thin end of the wedge, and the discussion was stopped.

Swivelling Simon was hanging the tea-bag up to dry near the stove, so he could enjoy a pinch of snuff later, when he began to fumble around with his good eye.

The drains Inspector asked if he was okay and Simon explained, "My lens shifted, that's all."

One lung Louie looked up, and said, "I didn't know you wore lenses."

Simon was slightly annoyed as he replied, "Not lenses, you buffoon, *lens*. What good is it wasting one on a glass eye? Mine last twice as long."

The gang were impressed. They knew he was mean, but there were obviously things they hadn't spotted yet.

"Have you got bubbles coming out of your eye?" asked Buster doubting his own eyesight.

"Oh, possibly," admitted Simon. "I'm trying out a new liquid solution for my lens."

The drains Inspector noted, "But it bubbles. What sort of solution bubbles?"

"Washing-up liquid," said Simon sheepishly.

The road gang studiously drank their tea. They were careful about the things they said to Simon because he was of the opinion that since he could manage with only one eye, he realised how many things could be saved if he used them properly.

The drains Inspector then jokingly suggested that if he leaned on one side as he drank, he would only use one kidney. This had resulted in Simon leaning over one arm of his chair for weeks and making the others feel seasick!

*

Marvin stood outside his office window and watched the road gang file inside. They seemed to have lost some of their spirit lately, but certainly none of their smell!

Marvin explained the situation. "Red Ronnie has stirred up a lot of unrest with his anti-authority attitudes lately. It has come from above that the answer is *Job-Rotation*."

The team gaped in disbelief as they stared over Marvin's shoulder at a file of secretaries moving past wearing tunnel overalls, masks, bright yellow gloves, and carrying buckets. *One was wearing stilettos!*

"But, but," stammered Buster, "We can't type."

"Can't wear those blooming shoes either," muttered the drains Inspector.

"Hurr, hurr," managed Louie, on the verge of collapse.

Marvin shook his head impatiently, "No, you lot have been given the job of inspecting this circus business; the bosses think you will blend in because animals can smell a human miles away."

The team slouched out through Cubicle-city, trying to salvage some good news from all this. No-one noticed that the cubicles were empty.

Back at the cabin and still distracted, Buster stepped out of the way and allowed Simon to enter first.

Simon stopped, turned and staggered back out, one eye swivelling wildly and the other bubbling like a cauldron. Refusing to open his mouth he then pulled his coat over his head and began to inhale deeply.

"Hyperventilating?" suggested the drains Inspector.

Buster tried, "Someone nicked his tea-bag?"

Louie advanced cautiously, put his head around the door and backed off, holding his eyes and breathing like a broken bellows. The drains Inspector and Buster exchanged glances. What could there possibly be in there to frighten men of this calibre?

Just as Buster disappeared inside, the word came to the Inspector. *Hygiene!*

Buster had to be led back outside like a child.

The drains Inspector had only peered through slitted eyes, but it was enough!

The cabin had been scoured. The cups gleamed. The fresh air smell caught in the throat, and there were flowers!

As he slammed the door to stop this abomination from escaping, the Inspector noticed a hand-written sign. T.A.R.T.S.

In smaller letters underneath was the explanation.

TYPIST'S **A**REA for **R**EST from **T**ENSION and **S**TRESS

Please wipe you feet

It was *over,* all those years of carefully laid grime, all that male bonding and dirty jokes. Enamel mugs didn't just appear with that patina on the inside, all gone. Chemically eradicated!

The dejected team dispersed.

Chapter 34

The hippo finished licking a particularly mature piece of wall and then moved on.

The penguins had popped-out to be fed as there weren't that many fish to be had down here. They had tried standing in a circle around some chap's fish-hook in a square room up the hill, but as he never caught anything it lengthened the odds for the penguins.

The hippo liked these solitary moments. He could practice his breathing techniques. If he breathed out too hard when he had company, the little fellers went down like skittles!

Cuthbert was really enjoying himself. He strode around the farmyard trying to crack his whip. Judging by the windows, shutters and cups, he had cracked everything but!

The animals certainly responded to him. As soon as he appeared they moved a respectful distance away. This was an improvement on turning their backs on him.

Percy wasn't around to watch. He was shifting and stacking bales of hay to mark out the perimeter of the ring inside the cinema. Every time anyone mentioned manual work now, Cuthbert pointed to his white trousers and raised an eyebrow. They soon went away.

The animals were becoming excited too. They recognised the preparations and began to exercise and try out little routines of their own. The gorilla didn't put himself out because his role as the primary primate involved squatting in a menacing fashion, and he was at the top of his game.

The elephant had begun to wonder where the hippo was. They had a grunted agreement to share the duck pond. One half of the day involved wallowing and the other half allowed bathing and showering. Lately, the elephant was in danger of becoming too clean! Even the penguins didn't appear very often now. The elephant vaguely wondered if the lesser species had actually died out without sensible tusks and big floppy ears. *Still, may as well have a shower,* he thought.

Percy had trundled his tractor up and down the hill all day with heavy bales for the circus ring. Things were really taking shape now but one niggling worry was that *he* didn't seem to have a costume, and the penguins weren't around to train for a routine.

115

Sitting on a hay bale with a cup of tea, he watched some of the women putting animals through their paces. Everyone had been really nice and thanked him for all his work building the ring, but there seemed to be a silence in the costume department. Feeling a presence beside him, Percy absently offered his cup to give his companion a drink.

After a noisy slurp the empty cup was handed back. Percy glanced down into the cup and refilled it from his flask, another slurp, another refill. Percy sat looking down at his feet as his wellies swung backwards and forwards below him. "Sometimes, I don't really feel part of all this," he said.

An arm dropped heavily on his shoulder in sympathy.

"Ooh look!" said Elspeth pointing at Percy and his companion, "Percy must have dressed as a gorilla and put his clothes on one of the chimps!"

Cuthbert was trying desperately to get the stains out of his white trousers before Margery spotted them. His whip-cracking had come on nicely until the giraffe had walked behind him. The long whip had spiralled around the long neck and the animal had bolted. Cuthbert had ended up back in the farmyard after a circuit of the hill. His trousers were no longer white and his top-hat was squashed like a folding opera hat. Punching it back into shape he managed to knock the top out, leaving it flapping like an opened can of beans!

Margery would not be pleased!

Cuthbert may be the ringmaster, but the organisation was in the hands of the Captain. An air traffic controller would have been proud of his schedule. Because the electrical supply was almost mythical, the Captain had devised a system of wires and pulleys to contact the backstage area, and all the animals wore a numbered plaque. He would attach a number to the wire, and by pulling hard the number would wobble its way backstage and the next act would be prepared.

The Valley Mafia 'Compost team' were keeping the place spotless, and they loaned a 'man' to the Captain as a communications motivator. He pulled the wire!

At last, thought Percy. He had been summoned to the dressing area. Without a glance, he patted his companion's furry knee and said, "Wish me luck," before slapping across the building.

The dressing area was full of people. Even Marvin and the road gang were there. Someone had very cleverly stood them at the wind

116

machine and turned it on! Percy managed to jump up and down whilst standing still, until Margery turned to him.

"Ahh, there you are Percy, sorry for the delay dear," and with a sweep of her arm indicated his costume.

Percy looked, blinked, and looked again. All he could see was a big pair of red boots and a false red nose. "That's it?" he asked.

"Cuthbert is as much use as a traffic cone at sea and he's dressed up like a dog's dinner, and this is all I get?" He narrowed his eyes and looked at Margery, "This is because I accidentally watered the plants in the Gents, isn't it?"

"**That was you**?" shrieked Margery.

Percy said quickly, "Er, no, of course not." He thought for a minute then tried, "It's because I wrecked the car, isn't it?"

"You wrecked my car?" shrieked Marvin.

"Er, not wrecked exactly," muttered Percy. "I know, I know," he said loudly, "It's because I filled in that form and you all received bondage catalogues, isn't it?"

Many faces turned in his direction and Percy gulped. Henry whispered to him urgently, "Wear the boots Percy, or you won't have anything to put your hat on!"

Percy wore the boots!

The gorilla brightened up when he saw Percy coming back.

The big red boots had altered his sound slightly. Because he had kept his wellies on as well, he now produced, *slap flop, slap flop,* wherever he went. Percy looked for his new companion, but all he could see was the gorilla. *Marvellous,* he thought, *You no sooner find a mate and he disappears!*

The gorilla watched sadly as Percy went the other way.

Outside, there were several coaches full of tourists. They were invited because every circus needs to generate an atmosphere. They were filing in just as Percy walked by, followed by a line of inquisitive monkeys.

"Oh look," said Ronald sarcastically, "It's the Messiah and his disciples."

Percy growled, "Don't kid yourself mate, they weren't all disciples. Some only started following after he turned water into wine."

A passing parent clapped her hands over her child's ears and shrieked, "*Bad clown*, you'll go straight to hell!"

Percy paused to ask, "Madam, I'm wearing a false nose, floppy

117

boots, and I live with Cuthbert. What else can they threaten me with?"

Henry was in charge of spotlights and music. He gradually dimmed the lights as the audience settled down. The judges were seated and the Captain signalled that all was ready. A single spot shone onto the centre of the ring.

Cuthbert stood like a caricature. With the top of his hat flapping, muddy knees and a broken whip, he looked more like Baron Samedi in a bad voodoo movie, than the ringmaster about to take on the world. The spotlight widened out and encompassed Marjorie, billowing in feathers leading her troupe of ponies, horses, and the llama.

All the animals circled the ring keeping as much room between themselves and Cuthbert as they could. Margery certainly didn't trust herself anywhere near him.

Next on was the elephant pulling the lion's cage. The elephant flapped his ears and the lion paced menacingly.

Percy appeared next. He was festooned with water balloons and had been encouraged to throw them at the audience. *This was more like it*, he thought, snapping the thin thread holding a balloon and hurling it at Cuthbert. Somehow, it came straight back and soaked him.

The crowd roared; they loved it!

Trying again with the same result, Percy was simply getting wetter. That's when he realised that the Valley Mafia had also fastened the balloons with lengths of elastic!

Running over to Cuthbert, Percy lifted the top flap of the ringmaster's hat and dropped a water balloon inside; then began a keystone kops chase around the ring as Percy tried to burst it.

Next into the ring came Arkle. The crowd roared its approval, until they realised that it was the gorilla behind her who was the actual feature.

Elspeth came next with the elegant giraffe. The creature was well used to this and dipped its head into the audience so that the children could see those dark brown eyes.

Next came Avril with the penguins, she was dressed as a drum major and threw her baton into the air as the birds waddled faithfully behind her.

Belinda came out next, releasing pure white doves into the air along with one black crow. He looked rather like an apostrophe

118

amongst them.

The next event had the crowd on its feet. Ronald thundered into the ring in full cowboy gear, mounted on a white stallion. Drawing his six-gun, Ronald fired in various directions very quickly.

Almost simultaneously the balloon in Cuthbert's hat exploded, Percy's red nose flew across the ring, Avril's baton snapped in mid-air, and the lock flew off the lion's cage!

Henry stood and shouted to his brother, "I thought you were firing blanks?"

Ronald wheeled his horse around dramatically, "Blanks, what are *those*?"

The lion stopped pacing and gave his door an experimental flick. *It opened*!

The giraffe caught sight of the lion putting one paw outside its cage and headed for the exit, its long neck catching on the wire carrying the Captain's numbers across the building.

"Ooh LOOK!" shouted the children as the member of the Valley Mafia hurtled across ceiling still holding on tight. "It's Peter Pan," cried the audience.

Another member of the Valley Mafia, conscious of his contract with the cucumber factory, dashed across the ring with a bucket and cannoned into Arkle. Arkle didn't even notice, but the bucket went up into the air and landed upside down on the gorilla's head. Now, an angry gorilla is noisy at the best of times, but magnified by a bucket it is really awesome! And the bass beat of fists on a big hollow chest really made the hairs on the neck stand up. The lion, not to be outdone, began with a rattle in his throat and ended with a splitting crescendo of a roar.

Everyone looked at the cage and one by one they realised that it wasn't where the noise was coming from! Cuthbert saw the lion padding dangerously across the ring. He moved towards it *This is it,* he thought, *This is where the ringmaster cracks his whip and drives the savage beast back into its cage and saves the day.*

Percy saw the lion padding dangerously across the ring and thought almost exactly the same as Cuthbert. *This is a job for the ringmaster, not the clown.* He ran away.

Mrs. Biggle watched the lion padding dangerously across the ring. She thought about the children behind her, who thought this was part of the act. Reaching into her bag for the mobile phone she picked up her

119

powder compact by mistake, and called the Police.

The lion disappeared in a cloud of Jungle Blush, and the children cheered. By the time Cuthbert reached the scene Arkle had dragged the coughing sneezing lion back into its cage and twisted the gate shut.

Mrs. Biggle caught Cuthbert's eye, and said, "That's why your Aunt said, *Mind the lion dear,* it has terrible asthma!"

The crowd was jumping up and down, the children were mesmerised and the judges were ticking boxes as fast as they found them.

Margery led the furry animals in a salute to the crowd with the ponies bending a knee. The gorilla had removed the bucket and was sitting on it. Or, everyone hoped that he was just sitting on it!

Behind the line up of animals facing the crowd, a trapdoor opened slowly and the hippo appeared, blinking into the light.

The crowd gasped and fell silent in wonder. The hippo began to hum and the penguins moved into place around it. They stood and swayed as Bolero reverberated around the building, and as the hushed audience watched the hippo changed into a medley from Swan Lake performed by little fellers in dinner jackets.

The judges were stunned. This year the bar had been set higher than ever before, because some people didn't believe that the animals enjoyed performing. But here it was, the animals had won in spite of the humans!

In the wings Aunt Edith shed a silent tear.

Chapter 35

Back at The Mandrake Arms after the performance, the ladies had reluctantly changed out of their circus costumes. Everyone surrounded Aunt Edith and it was drinks all round.

Marjorie had been brooding for a while now, and she suddenly sat bolt upright. "The bell!" she exclaimed as she dashed outside.

Arkle tutted, "Show business goes straight to some people's heads, she thinks she's the Hunchback of Notre Dame now."

They all wandered out to where Marjorie was rubbing the bell as if expecting a genie to appear, "Look, look," she said, "My sound is silver when I'm tolled. Though made of bronze, my heart is gold." She looked wildly around at her audience. "It's the bell, that's where Aunt Edith hid her gold; it was cast into the bell."

"Did I?" asked Aunt Edith. "I don't remember that."

"But, but …" stammered Marjorie.

Edith relented somewhat and led Marjorie to a seat. "Tales of successful business and great wealth have followed me all my life," she said.

"Why's that?" asked Avril.

"Well, because I was very successful at business and very wealthy I suppose, but don't think that a circus is cheap to run you know. All those animals do all day is make a mess and eat everything in sight, bit like running a men's hostel really."

Marjorie was deflated, "So there's no gold then?"

Edith patted her arm, "Not over here dear, the gnomes of Zurich look after it for me."

The ladies wandered back inside and Elspeth was heard to mutter, "Shame, we could have bought Cuthbert some curtains."

Percy lay on his back at the top of the hill. It was the ultimate type of day to watch the clouds.

Oddly enough, Cuthbert refused point-blank to accompany him these days. Percy had no idea why, now what was that floating towards him?

~ The End ~

121

About the Author

Patrick Barrett is a sixty year old ex-miner from Mansfield in Nottinghamshire. He is married to Paula and between them, they have several children. 'Shakespeare's Cuthbert' was his first book, though he has been writing comedy for several years.

His aims as a writer are 'to be successful and make people laugh by providing them with an escape from the harshness of real life'.

His other abiding interest is in antiques.